Book of the Dead

A Horror Anthology By New And Established Writers

Black Hart Entertainment

Edinburgh. Scotland

First published 2018.

Black Hart Entertainment.
32 Glencoul Ave, Dalgetty Bay, Fife KY11 9XL.
cityofthedeadtours.com

Cover by Jan-Andrew Henderson.

Edited by Black Hart Entertainment.

Book Layout © 2017 BookDesignTemplates.com

Book of the Dead. 1st ed.
ISBN 978-0-9928561-1-3 (print)
ISBN 978-0-9928561-2-0 (eBook)

Contents

Foreword

This book came from an odd place - and we don't mean Dundee. Black Hart Entertainment run *City of the Dead* Ghost Tours in Edinburgh, so it may seem strange that we're publishing a horror anthology. Then again, scaring people, is our business. So, we thought it would be fun to organise a writing competition and publish the best stories by new writers, along with some more well-established authors.

Our aim was simple. Spread a little terror around.

Fittingly, several of our contributions come from Scotland, though there are also entries from the rest of the UK, as well as Ireland, the USA, Germany and Australia. They weren't picked by a panel of experts but by ordinary people who happen to be horror aficionados. Who better? Nor did we stick to traditional tropes or subjects. There are no vampires or zombies and some of the stories are funny. As long as you consider death amusing.

So, welcome to *Book of the Dead*. Here's hoping it keeps you up all night.

Even after you've finished reading it...

Bunny Wunny Woo

J A H e n d e r s o n

A few years ago, I took part in an anti-war march on Glasgow's Buchanan Street. Or maybe it was pro-war. I was nipping out of the office for a cheese roll so I was only in it for 5 minutes.

Being lunchtime, most of the sandwich makers were on their break and they'd taken up the entire window watching the parade. A police horse had done its business all over the road and they were taking bets about who would stand in it first. My money was on the guys on stilts dressed as Death.

Suddenly there was a huge cheer from the window. A girl in a wheelchair had gone right through the mess. The workers in the sandwich shop went wild, cheering and waving at her.

That's when I decided to become an entertainer.

I quit my job in sales and enrolled at Dunfermline College of Drama. It used to be a polytechnic, teaching joiners and the like and I think they kept some of the old lecturers. I was taught wooden acting and spent a lot of time being a tree.

My gamble paid off, however. I got an agent within seven years of graduating and a few months after that moved into TV roles. I was 'woman in fish van' in *Monarch of the Glen* and 'irate deaf mute who falls over' in *River City*, though you can only see my feet stuck up in the air. Eventually I got typecast as 'dead body in bath' in dozens of crime series on account of my natural resistance to wrinkling, even after hours lying motionless in cold water.

Then, just as I was sure my big break was around the corner I ended up getting pregnant. I'd dreamed of marrying my childhood sweetheart, but I didn't have one, so I ended up with a childhood acquaintance instead.

When little Bryant was born I took him with me to one of my acting jobs - playing 'body found in dumpster' in an episode of *Taggart*. The director spotted Bryant and cast him as 'plain baby in pram'. He ended up in four scenes, got a bigger cheque than me and wasn't even a member of Equity.

That kind of success eluded my husband, who was a struggling horror writer. He cast me in his plays a lot, so it was handy I had plenty of experience playing dead. Even so, it's hard to lie on the floor for an hour at an Edinburgh Fringe performance, staring sightlessly at an audience of seven who look more lifeless than you.

We didn't give up though. The glass is either half empty or half full. In the end, we emptied and filled it quite a bit, which probably didn't help our careers much.

In the last few months, however, my husband seemed to be going through a self-improvement phase. He became more assured. His hair had developed white flecks, prominent at the temples. Wisely, he cut it short but not cropped like someone who hadn't the imagination to do anything else. Didn't grow a goatee for compensation. He looked good. Better than when I met him.

One night, as we drank wine, he said

"Sometimes I feel I'm a character in one of my own stories. I can make myself do this or that but it's like I'm describing my feelings rather than experiencing them." He drained his glass. "Maybe I should stop writing and start living."

I nodded, not daring to jump on the idea while my husband was still deciding if it was safe to climb up. Also, I couldn't tell if he was being serious or thinking of lines for a new play.

The next week he came home with Bunny Wunny Woo.

"...And what is that?"

It was upside down on one of the pine kitchen chairs. Its head hung over the seat, black nappy candy-floss hair, dusting the floor. The arms dangled in mock surrender or a gravity defying handstand, bent awkwardly at elbow and wrist. Its head was too big for the malnourished wooden body and the jaw was twisted and splintered as if some almighty haymaker had propelled it over the back of the seat and into its present position. Now it lay unconscious or stunned or dead. Its eyes should have been closed or crossed or sightlessly staring so I could tell which.

But it didn't have eyes, only empty sockets.

"This," said my husband. "Is Bunny Wunny Woo."

"Is it now?" I replied.

My husband hasn't really paid the attention to our son that I'd like. Not the sort, I suppose. He never had a pet in his life and, as far as I know, doesn't remember to water plants.

He sometimes joked about his reluctance to hold Bryant.

"There's nothing to the little man yet. Doesn't seem quite real."

He didn't say it like he expected anything to change.

He'd brought home toys for Bryant before, though I often wondered if that was a just a way of keeping him quiet Bunny Wunny Woo was different. The broken body would need a lot of work and have to be repainted.

But Bunny Wunny Woo wasn't *for* Bryant.

"I've got a great idea for a horror play," my husband said.

"I take it the dummy will feature heavily."

"Absolutely!" He held up the manikin. "Ventriloquist dolls are innately creepy."

This one was. Nothing innate about it. My husband seemed pleased by that

"I like him."

"I hate it."

"Either way, you can't ignore him, eh?"

"Where did you get the little fucker?" I asked.

"Found him in a skip," my husband said. "I'm going to fix him. I'll learn how to do the voice."

"Ventriloquism?"

"Why not?"

"It looks like someone beat him up."

"I'll speak for him. I'll sort him."

"Where'd he get that stupid name?"

My husband pulled back the dummy's collar, revealing a scrawny unpainted wooden neck.

"It's written on a tag."

He wiggled Bunny Wunny Woo's head at me. The broken jaw bounced slackly, held only by a couple of loose gut tendons. My husband spoke out of the side of his mouth.

How do you do?
I'm Bunny Wunny Woo
My eyes are broken
My jaw is too
But I'll get fixed and be good as new.

"Very impressive, honey."

My husband began writing his play. He seemed confident that this would be a big success. He hired a room with a stage in Wilkie House, down in the Cowgate. Got some flyers made up advertising the show. I argued that Bunny Wunny Woo wasn't a very creepy name for a horror play, but my husband was adamant.

"It'll get people wondering," he said.

"Yeah. About your sanity."

To be honest, the plot was pretty standard stuff. About a ventriloquist dummy that slowly takes over a family. I played the mother who, of course, ends up dying. My husband played the husband who doesn't notice anything is wrong.

Nothing like a bit of typecasting.

My husband began to fix up Bunny Wunny Woo, as promised. He got a set of false teeth, cut a bit to size, and painted it the same colour as the face. I watched him shape and paint and attach it, half impressed, half bored. And with an indefinable fraction of unease. He had bought a large gooey rubber eye from the joke shop. It was a bounce ball or one of those things you throw at the wall and it sticks. He cut it in half and glued them into the empty sockets.

"There we go."

The eyeballs glared. My husband put his hand inside Bunny Wunny Woo's jacket. The jaw clicked open and shut like a little piranha, expression wide and emotionless.

"It looked creepy before. Now it would give Charley Manson nightmares."

How do you do?
I'm Bunny Wunny Woo
My eyes are starey
My jaw is scary
But I'm not as hairy as my Auntie Mary

The jaw moved rather well. My husband's lips moved too, rather obviously. He looked at Bunny Wunny Woo's blank face and I looked at his.

"What? I'm still working on it."

I admit, the lines of his new play were better than usual. Easy to learn, even if there were a lot of them. By two days before the show, I had them three quarters down. All good actresses do it that way.

"You remember I agreed to look after William tomorrow afternoon?" I asked as my husband paced the floor, biting his nails. "While I'm going over my lines."

William is my sister's boy, a quiet little thing. If I'm honest, he's a bit slow. In a way, looking after him is rehearsal too, for when Bryant gets older. I suppose you could call it life imitating life.

"Tell him not to mess with Bunny Wunny Woo," my husband pleaded.

"I doubt he'd touch it if I gave him a barge pole."

"Claire, he's just a dummy," my husband said huffily. "What harm can he do to anyone?"

William arrived next afternoon. My lines weren't *quite* learned yet. Bunny Wunny woo wasn't entirely mended. My husband had gone for a walk because the house wasn't big enough to contain his pacing.

William was no trouble to look after, though. I knew he liked art, it must run in the family, so I'd bought some crayons and a pad for him at the Spar. When he arrived Bunny Wunny Woo was sitting in my husband's chair, legs sticking straight out. William gave a little start.

Bunny Wunny Woo had splints fastened to his broken arms. My husband had applied glue to the snapped limbs and the woods kept everything in place while it dried. He looked like he was strapped in an electric chair, sitting like that.

I put a large tartan blanket on the floor for William to kneel on.

"Here's a colouring book," I smiled. "Aunt Claire's got some work to do, so she's going to the kitchen."

I went next door. Got my script out. Did a few vocal exercises and resisted the temptation to practice being dead. I couldn't work with Bunny Wunny Woo until his glue dried so I put an old sock over my hand instead.

Stand in for ventriloquist dummy. I knew how the sock felt.

I felt a tug at my leg. It was William.

"The big doll lookin at me." His eyes were tearful.

"The big doll can't harm you, honey."

"I don' like it. Scary lookin at me."

"His name's Bunny Wunny Woo."

"Bun oh oh. Oh."

"That's right. Aunt Claire's a bit busy right now."

"S'awright."

He turned and waddled off, back to the living room.

How do you do?
I'm Bunny Wunny Woo
With eyes to see
And a jaw to chew
Now we've gotten in a stew
You fixed me and I'll fix you.

There was another tug at my leg.

"Big doll talkin to me. Scare me."

"William," I sighed. "Aunt Claire is very busy."

"Take big doll away."

"What's the doll saying?"

"Don' know."

"Aunt Claire can't move Bunny Wunny Woo until his glue dries. He's not going to harm you."

"S'ugly. Scary."

"William. You can colour in right here. On the floor. You go and get your blanket and bring it, but you *can't* disturb Aunt Claire."

William looked tearful again.

"Tell you what." I said brightly. "Why don't you take your blanket and put it over Bunny Wunny Woo! Then you can't see him. And he can't see you."

William padded back into the living room.

I started back on the lines

C'mon, he's just a dummy, what harm can he do to anyone?

I dropped my script and ran to the living room, skidding on the polished kitchen floor as I went.

Bunny Wunny Woo was sitting on my husband's chair, mouth open, staring with its dead fish eyes. William was on the floor scribbling furiously.

Bryant's crib was in the corner, his motionless body covered by a large tartan blanket.

William didn't look up.

"Ugly doll can't see me any more," he said.

Jan-Andrew Henderson is the author of 23 non-fiction and fiction books, has been published in the UK, USA, Canada, Germany, Australia and The Czech Republic and is winner of the Royal Mail and Doncaster Book Awards. He divides his time between Edinburgh, Scotland and Brisbane, Australia

Lambent Lights

H R Boldwood

I t is true. There is no rest for the wicked. This morn, I awoke to a symphony of saws and hammers that heralded the raising of my gallows. No doubt by midday the news had spread through the city more quickly than consumption. The Graveyard Ghoul to swing! Ian Bates dies on the morrow! Surely, the merchants of Baltimore bustled in the streets, hawking their wares like draggletailed harlots. Sundries for the hanging! Parasols for the ladies - hats for the gents - penny candy for the babes.

I'll wager that upon the lighting of the street lamps the town cronies raised a toast to my impending demise. So quick they are to see me dangle at the end of a rope…and so blind to the truth.

Moonlight bleeds through the iron bars of my cell, spilling across first one stone and then the next, pursuing me relentlessly. I conceal myself in the shadows, certain beyond all reason that the Angel Gideon, sword held high, rides that light like a stallion. Patient as Job, he is, waiting to pass judgment upon me.

Without question and for just cause, I shall be found lacking. But I should not stand alone. Let me be clear. It is not forgiveness I seek whilst idling in the shadow of the hangman's noose.

It is vengeance against the demon seed that put me here.

It was well past midnight on June 3, 1830, when wearied by my duties as night watchman at The Westminster Hall and Burying Ground, I leaned against the carriage gates to enjoy a paste cigar and partake in some mindless wool-gathering. From the corner of my eye, I spied a lambent light at the edge of the property.

Having served as the cemetery's watchman for nearly a decade, I speak with great authority on the matter of these mystifying lights. These ghostly will-o'-the-wisps are sentient beings, at best mercurial, at worst malignant and have lured many a man to his damnation.

We both ply our trades in the dead of night, these lights and I. In that regard we are kindred, and so afford each other easement as we go about our business. Given the fickle nature of these fiery sprites, I am wont to grant them a wide berth.

However, on this particular night, the shimmering spectre beckoned me, refusing me respite until I answered its call. Senses keen and nerves atingle, I grabbed a mucking shovel from the gateway and proceeded into the burying grounds.

Then came an unexpected sound that chilled me to the bone. It was a nearly imperceptible ringing in the distance.

Steady now, I thought, 'tis likely your ears deceive you, nothing more.

I continued on my way to where I'd seen the ghost light, whence came the sound again, only stronger. Without question, it was a bell with resonance and reverberation and not the result of fitful hallucination.

My heart thundered.

To a watchman on duty, a knelling in the night carried horrific implications -implications that brought me to shudder that very eve.

The ringing magnified one hundredfold - a banging, clanging, pealing appeal; a demanding, commanding call to action that could not be denied. Upon discovering its source, I stopped in place.

The sound that had beckoned me was the tolling of a safety bell from atop a freshly dug grave! I drove the mucking shovel deep and threw the dirt aside, scarcely allowing myself to consider the untenable truth.

The occupant of this grave was still alive.

"I'm coming!" I screamed. "Hold fast!"

The shovel, far too small for the task, was the only tool at hand. Faster and harder I shovelled and heaved, calling out, "I am almost there!" Soon, I heard a muffled thumping from beneath the dirt, and moments thereafter a frantic voice screamed from within the coffin.

Breathless, and with arms that had given their all, I raised the shovel high and brought it down like the hammer of Zeus upon the lock, breaking it free. I threw back the lid to the casket. Its occupant sprang upright like a demented jack-in-the-box!

Ne'er in my life had I seen such a sight. The man gulped air as if to inhale the sky; his eyes so wide they might have popped, his skin paler than a blood-less corpse. The cord that stretched from inside his coffin to the bell above ground remained in his hand. Adrift in a fugue, he continued to yank it reflexively, causing the bell to toll again and again. One by one, I pried his fingers free. He grabbed at me with such forceful desperation as to dislodge the buttons from my jacket. A croup-like cough burst from within his chest. I handed him my handkerchief and waited for his lungs to clear before moving him.

Once stabilised, I led the exhausted man to the caretaker's shanty and placed him in a chair beside the desk. He shivered in spite of the warm summer night. I laid my jacket across his shoulders, and he began to babble.

"God bless you, sir. Thank heaven you appeared! I hadn't long left. You saved me from a fate more grue-some than I could ever have imagined. My name is

Angus Winchell. How may I repay you? I don't even know your name."

"I am Ian Bates, the watchman of Westminster Hall," I said. "You're safe now, Mr. Winchell. I suggest you rest and pull your wits about you. Perhaps then you will explain how you came to be … buried alive."

I shuddered at the sound of those words, pulled a flask (reserved for medicinal purposes) from my back pocket and poured him a shot. It vanished, as did the next. So pallid he was, with eyes that looked feverish and over-bright.

"Mr. Bates, I assure you, I am of sound mind despite what you may come to think. Mine is a preposterous tale that defies all explanation; still, it is the truth. I will swear to it on my mother's grave."

"How utterly appropriate," I said, taking a goodly swig from the flask. Leaning back in my chair, I placed my feet atop the desk and sighed. "This entire episode defies explanation, Mr. Winchell. The prospect of a more implausible tale boggles the mind."

"There could be no story without Malcolm Fletcher," he began, "the most villainous lout ever slipped from a mother's loins. I rue the day I met the double-crossing bastard. We shared a coach and several bottles of whiskey while travelling from Charleston to Baltimore. He was a bright man, affable enough when he was in his cups, but as fate would have it a taciturn tyrant when abstinent.

The fool that I am formed a partnership with him before his sobriety surfaced. We opened The Winchell Fletcher Trading Company." He raised his brows. "Perhaps you know of it?"

I shook my head and he continued.

"Fletcher saw to the daily operations. I avoided him like the plague, simply supplying the capital as needed. We split the profits evenly. All was well and good, until he decided he no longer needed my money and wanted to buy me out."

"The thankless bugger!" said I.

"Wasn't he, though? I told him absolutely not, and if he did not agree, it would be I who bought him out. We did not speak for days, then suddenly he appeared in my office, hat in hand, offering me a glass of Hermitage Burgundy. He admitted that he had wronged me and lamented his odious behaviour. Tired of the quarrel, I accepted his apology. We toasted and agreed to allow bygones be bygones. But moments later, I fell ill.

"My sight blurred, and my belly boiled as if brimming with acid. I twitched like a festering corpse. Numbness quickly spread, beginning in my extremities, then progressing to my core. Unable to breathe, I collapsed. My last waking moment found Fletcher straddling me, flashing a serpentine twist of rotted teeth. His words chilled me to the quick.

"By now, you realize there was poison in your glass. But do not despair, Winchell. It will all be over soon; and then you will become fodder for the worms. Pity. This was all so unnecessary. You should have accepted my offer.'"

"When next I opened my eyes, I was surrounded by obsidian darkness, confined so that my head could barely raise, my arms and legs pinned alongside me. Thoughts muddled in my aching head, but when the veil of confusion lifted, my dilemma became morbidly clear. Reason departed and madness ensued. Screams pierced my ears. How terrified was I to discover the screams were mine!

"The more panic prevailed the less air remained. I found the cord and pulled, praying the bell would be heard." Winchell's voice cracked. "I was about to give up hope when suddenly, you appeared like an angel. I owe you my life."

"But the poison!" I cried. "How did you survive?"

Winchell gave a wry smile. "I can only surmise that Fletcher had a less than optimal grasp of alchemy."

"Astonishing!"

"I ask you, Mr. Bates, has ever a more horrific torture been inflicted upon a man than Malcolm Fletcher visited upon me?"

Opportunity dangled before me like low-hanging fruit. I seized the moment.

"Mr. Winchell, this Fletcher character as much as killed you. Consider the torment he wreaked upon you. Justice must be served."

He hesitated as if pondering my words.

"Aye, but what justice? What punishment befits so heinous a crime?"

"Why, death, of course! Swift, merciless, and discreet."

Winchell's eyes grew wide. "What are you implying, sir?"

"Biblical equity. An eye for an eye." I pulled my Barlow knife from my boot and thrust it to the tip of his chin. "Justice dispatched by the very angel that delivered you from the jaws of death. Even God could find no quarrel with that."

Winchell gulped. "You would...perform... such a service?"

"With proper motivation, it is possible."

"Money is no object, Mr. Bates, if that be what motivates you."

I wet my lips and in leaned close. "Do tell."

"What say you to twenty guineas?"

"Twenty guineas? To the man who pulled you from the worms? Surely, you can—"

"Fifty! Fifty guineas are yours. You have only to accept."

Not wishing to appear eager, I brought the discussion to a close. "There would be significant risk involved with such an endeavour. I shall take the matter under advisement."

Winchell gathered his legs beneath him and moved toward the door.

"Consider my offer, Mr. Bates. Surely, a watchman like yourself could make use of such a tidy sum. I shall meet you at the carriage gates tomorrow at midnight expecting your response. I leave you now to your conscience."

Odd, that he assumed I had a conscience. I am not now, nor have I ever been, a virtuous man. The road to hell may be paved with good intentions, but its stones are aflame with avarice. I have spent my lifetime skipping across those red-hot coals. Truth be told, this would not be my first undertaking of a nefarious nature. I have done dark and damnable things. My services are available - but always at a cost.

True to his word, Winchell approached the gates at the stroke of twelve the following eve.

"What say you, Bates?"

"Aye. I will do as you ask. But the cost is sixty guineas. Up front."

"Ridiculous! That's highway robbery."

"Perhaps. But there is something more I want."

Winchell's face blazed. "More, you cheeky bastard? What more could there be?"

"You must leave Baltimore. There can be no one to tie this deed back to me.'"

"You needn't worry about that, Bates. Once you have completed your duties, I will raid the coffers of The Winchell Fletcher Trading Company and disappear like smoke in the night. I will give you half the bounty now and the balance upon completion of your mission. You are experienced in these matters. Surely, you understand I would be a fool to pay you in full, only to have you renege. That would never do. Are we agreed?"

"We are," I said, with a vigorous shake of his hand.

"Listen carefully. Fletcher is as round as a barrel and hasn't a hair on his head. He walks with a decided limp and carries a gold tipped cane."

Winchell bit his lip and fidgeted with the cuff of his sleeve.

"I do not wish to tell you how to do your business; however, I might make a small suggestion. He is as predictable as the moon. Each night, he stops at The Cork and Stein to wallow in his nightly bottle of scotch. When he leaves at closing, he stumbles down Alesford Alley toward his home on Beaumont Street. Alesford is dark and quite secluded. The perfect place for misadventure."

His voice softened,

"Tomorrow night report for your shift as usual. Slip from the burying grounds unnoticed and secret yourself in the alley before the tavern closes. Commit the deed and abscond under cover of night. No one will be the wiser. You have no ties to the man. With a modicum of care, you shall ne'er be discovered."

I nodded my approval.

"Good man," he said, clapping my shoulder. He placed the money in my hand. "I shall meet you here at the gates at 3 a.m., with the balance of your bounty. Until then." Winchell tipped his hat and walked away, fading like a phantom in the night.

I finished my rounds and left the cemetery at shift's end to spend the day plotting the commission of my crime.

At one o'clock the following morning, I skulked, Barlow knife in hand, through the barren streets of Baltimore. The mouth of Alesford Alley yawned like a bottomless abyss before me. I picked my way through a sea of garbage and inhaled a bitter blend of urine and vomit. A discarded stack of crates offered suitable concealment.

Finally, Fletcher stumbled into the alley and wandered past my hiding place. I snatched him from behind, clamped my free hand over his mouth, and drove the blade deep into his back. He gurgled as his lungs filled with blood. Death took him quickly. I dropped his body in place and emptied his pockets as if he had been waylaid.

While scurrying from the scene, my heart near skipped a beat at the sight of a flickering light that danced at the end of the alley. The muffled sound of a child's cough caused me to sigh in relief. No doubt some guttersnipe warmed himself 'ore a pile of smouldering tinder. I stifled a curse and chastised myself. Every flicker becomes a ghost-light. Your nerves betray you, Nancy Boy.

I hurried back to the burying ground and counted the minutes until my meeting with Winchell. He did not arrive at three o'clock as agreed, and so, I continued to count the minutes until four. When still he had not arrived, my heart began to race. Having no recourse, I waited and watched the clock strike five. Winchell was nowhere to be found. I bellowed and shook the carriage gates is if to tear them asunder. Whence came six o'clock, the end of my shift, I travelled home both furious and baffled by his absence. Exhausted, I collapsed into bed where I tossed and turned until sleep claimed me.

Soon after, I awakened to a knock upon my door. It was Constable Hightower. He questioned my whereabouts the previous evening. It seemed a local businessman had been murdered in Alesford Alley.

I leaned against the doorjamb and yawned.

"I was in the commission of my duties as watchman at Westminster Hall, as I am every night."

His eyes narrowed. "Perhaps you arrived for work but left during the night."

"I assure you, I did not. Why would you suggest such a thing?"

"It appears the criminal left behind some evidence." He swept past me into the parlour. "We found a handkerchief."

"And?"

"It bears the monogram, IMB. Ian Michael Bates. That is your name, is it not?"

"Yes, of course, but I have no embroidered handkerchiefs. They are far too costly. Clearly, this belongs to some other man who shares those same initials."

"I considered that myself, you see," said the constable, "until I saw your coat hanging on the banister. Its buttons are missing."

I followed his eyes, first toward the coat, then down into the palm of his opened hand that held two buttons identical to those on my coat.

An ugly picture began to emerge. My teeth clenched as I recalled Winchell tearing at me from the grave, ripping those buttons free. The memory of handing him my handkerchief nearly brought me to my knees. The swine! He had likely paid some scullery maid to stitch my initials on my own handkerchief.

But why was Winchell set to frame me, when I could so easily point the finger of guilt to him? He must have had an accomplice. Someone had to bury him. But who?

An even darker question lurked in the corner of my mind, a question too unsettling for thoughtful deliberation. Before I ever heard the ringing of that damnable bell, I had been lured toward Winchell's grave by the ghost lights. I believed them to be colleagues, if not allies. Might they have betrayed me and lured me to my doom? If so, they could rest assured I would not go quietly.

Once taken into custody, I sung like a canary, quick to implicate Winchell. I even took the constable to the cemetery and showed him Winchell's grave, but it now contained the body of a woman who had been buried more than two weeks past!

Dear God! Had he displaced the poor woman's body for want of an open grave? Clearly, he reasoned I would hear the bell and dig him up. He must have returned the woman's body to the ground whilst I was dispatching Fletcher. Such depravity eluded even me.

Unwilling to yield, I demanded that the constable investigate The Winchell Fletcher Trading Company. To my dismay, he found no record of either Angus Winchell or such a company having ever existed in Baltimore. Malcolm Fletcher, the man I murdered, had been the owner of a local milling operation.

"Impossible!" I screamed, punching a hole in the wall of my cell. Who was this monster that so sorely fixed my fate? Why had he driven me to murder?

I dropped to my knees baffled and beaten certain only of having been duped.

Humiliation haunted me, but curiosity consumed me. What had this demon gained from his manipulations? It occurred to me that I may never know. And therein lay madness.

As if the nails in my coffin were insufficient, at trial, Fletcher's wife, Madilyn, a winsome woman with a heart-shaped face, drowned the judge with tears from her emerald eyes. Other than my testimony, I had little by way of defence. The court's decision came quickly and without mercy.

Thus, it comes to pass in this eleventh hour that I, a dead man walking, still grasp for the answer to this gruesome riddle.

The sun has yet to rise and already an angry mob demands its pound of flesh. I climb the gallows' steps to oblige them. From atop the platform, I scan the sea of faces on the ground below, finding not a benevolent soul among them.

But he is there, the monster I knew as Winchell, standing among the horde. His eyes lock with mine and a wicked grin consumes his face. He turns to the woman beside him and brushes his lips against her hair. She tilts her head upward, triumph beaming from her heart-shaped face. It is Mrs. Fletcher; her emerald eyes no longer brimming with tears as they had in court but with forbidden love for the man at her side.

The irony is sweet. I, the instrument of their duplicity, will swing alone.

As the noose slips o'er my head, I catch a fleeting glimpse of the will-o'-the-wisps migrating through the early morning fog, their tiny flickers burning brighter, closer. They come to claim my blackened soul, for God above will not.

The trap door opens and at the snap of the rope I am transformed. I no longer fear the wrath of Gideon's sword. I no longer seek the solace of shadows.

I am a lambent light seen from the corner of the eye, a flickering harbinger of doom, waiting for the cur who ruined me to breathe his last. He will see my flame glowing in the distance, moving ever closer, blazing ever hotter until it swallows him whole.

And I will revel as I descend into the bowels of hell, dragging his wretched soul behind me - for vengeance will be mine.

H.R. Boldwood writes horror and speculative fiction. In another incarnation, she is a Pushcart Prize nominee, awarded the 2009 Bilbo Award for creative writing. Credits include, *Killing it Softly*, **Sho**rt *Story America*, *Bete Noir*, *Hyperion and Theia Volume One*, *Toys in the Attic*, *Floppy Shoes Apocalypse II*, *Pilcrow and Dagger* **and** *Sirens Call*.

The story Lambent Lights first appeared in *Ealain Magazine* **in 2015 and again in** *Killing It Softly Volume 1* **2016.**

www.hrboldwood.com

https://buff.ly/2tQFaYS

Mr Quibbly's Brain Emporium

Ishbelle Bee

I f you throw a human brain at a wall, it will splat against the wall and then drop onto the floor. And THAT gentleman, is all we can be certain of.

(Professor Izoltzkerzimm – The World's Leading Neurologist, speaking at the annual research conference in Munich 1883, on the mystery of the human mind, after an excessive amount of Pina Coladas.)

Mr Quibbly's Brain Emporium, Cat Gut Alley, 1885. Edinburgh

I am unique, for I am the only brain harvester in the city. Acquiring them is a relatively simple task. I loiter within the shadow-soup of gloomy alleyways and smack the individual, unwittingly donating their brain, over the head with a shovel.

Whilst unconscious, I drag em into a wheelbarrow, sling a potato sack over them and wheel them off to my little shop. There, I perform the necessary surgery (with a clamp, pair of forceps and a sink plunger) alleviating them of their cranial matter. The removed brain is plopped into a surgical jar of formaldehyde with a sprig of lavender. As a final touch, I tie a pink ribbon into a bow upon the jar and gum a label.

Quibbly's Brain Emporium
Harvested from the highest quality specimens

They are purchased as decorative arts, exotic paperweights and doorstoppers. Converted into table lamps. Often used as theatre props and séance parlour objects of horror. In my opinion, they are a wonderful feature on a mantelpiece, stimulating intriguing conversation. I imagine two gentlemen, after their supper, sucking over their cigars, with a glass of brandy in their hands.

"Oh, Mr Bilmes, what a marvellous brain you have displayed over the fireplace."

"Why thank you Mr Undershit. It was a remarkable find, acquired from a curious little brain emporium down a dubious back alley of Edinburgh. *Quibbly's* if I recall. He may have cornered the market, for I know of none other with the vision or daring-do to acquire and sell jars of pickled brains."

"It is a glorious thing. And under the illusion of candle light, it appears as if, a newly discovered variant of jellyfish. How it floats and stirs mysteriously within its glass confinement."

"Oh Mr Undershit, your mind is delightfully fertile. Perhaps your brain one day will be plopped within a jar of formaldehyde?"

"I certainly hope not."

"Come now. I think there are certain benefits to such a fate."

"Such as?"

"I must confess something to you. Something that you may consider shocking. I have ...succumbed to its whims."

"Whose whims?"

"The brain in the jar, Mr Undershit."

"I don't understand. What have you succumbed to?"

"The strange pleasures betwixt Man and Brain."

"You mean?!" (He gasps) "Surely that is unnatural?!"

"Tosh....tish tosh! It is perfectly natural for a civilised man to take a human brain to his bed chamber."

"Does Mrs Bilmes not object?"

"I have locked Mrs Bilmes in the outdoor privy, to avoid her opinion."

"I am feeling rather unwell."

"It is the shock of my revelation, Mr Undershit. Your undeveloped mind cannot fully comprehend what I have said to you."

"My legs are wobbly. I am rather confused."

"We are all confused Mr Undershit. Even I have questioned myself."

"Well, that's a small comfort."

"Questioned myself vigorously with the birch twigs. Thrashed myself stupid!"

"Is there any more brandy?"

"Help yourself dear friend. You need time to process what I have told you."

"I need a lot more alcohol."

"Ah, you were always frail Undershit. Always womanly in your sensibilities."

"I think you should let Mrs Bilmes out of the privy."

"All in good time. All in good time. She too, needs time to reflect upon my new companion. My little darling."

"It's a brain in a jar!"

"But it's so much more. If you could only see the connection we have together."

"I am trying not to imagine it. Please I beg you. Shut up."

I awaken myself from my daydream – slap the feather duster over the rows of jars.

Last week I smacked a literary agent over the head with the aforementioned shovel. The brain sadly was a diseased and poor sample, with an under-developed frontal lobe. I had to toss it into the bargain bucket, where it remains unsold.

My little brain emporium is situated on the Royal Mile of the great city of Edinburgh. She is a pale, slim Queen with a river of black hair. Her sister, the red headed Queen London lays below her, wide hipped and powerful. Both ladies like heads chopped off. Stuck on spikes. But it is I who must have the brains.

I hum a little tune while I dust the specimens. Quiet in their jars. Oh, what joy I take in my occupation! Oh, what felicity! I tap and point my slippered foot. I dance about the shop. Twirl the feather duster in spirals in the air. Imagine sparks fly and I am a magician. The brains begin singing in their jars, a celestial harmony of rising voices. A melody to make the angels daft in the head. Sing my darlings. Sing.

Outside it rains. Beats down upon the humanoids. Black water of great sadness. Fear. Poverty. Hunger. The weight of a million corpses.

But in my little shop we sing. We are music. We are joy and joy and joy.

Ishbelle Bee is an author & poet of fairy-tale horror & whimsy. Her work is inspired by folklore and mythology and set in alternate historical eras. She is particularly interested in exploring themes of metamorphosis, power and fairy-tale foods.

Her debut novel, *The Singular and Extraordinary Tale of Mirror and Goliath and The Contrary*

Tale of the Butterfly Girl, was published in 2015 by Angry Robot.

Her first poetry chapbook, *Blue Ink*, was published by Dancing Girl Press in 2017

The Tunnel

Catherine Macphail

I t was pouring with rain when they arrived. Five men from the Council, ready to work on the tunnel.

It ran under the canal. A shortcut to get from one side of the river to the other. But it hadn't been used for a long time and fell into disrepair. Now it was to be closed up completely.

There were rumours about strange things that had happened in the tunnel. No one believed the stories, of course, but nobody took the shortcut anymore.

Willie Tosh was the foreman.

"Gordon, you and Sharkey go through and begin to seal off the other end."

"I don't really want to go in there." Gordon stood back. "Had a bad experience in that tunnel."

"Och no' you as well, Gordon," Willie sighed. "These tales, they're all a load of rubbish."

"I've never actually been in there." This was Sharkey, big bull of a guy. He worked as a bouncer at the weekend in one of the local clubs. "I've just heard the stories. Spooky stories. I wouldn't mind seeing inside for myself."

He shrugged. "Come on Gordon. I'll look after you."

Willie laughed. "Nothing'll happen to you when you're wi a big guy like Sharkey."

"I'm no' making this up." Gordon shook his head. "I've been in there. You can hear things. You think somebody's following you. Even when the lights are working, it's always dark."

There were no lights in the tunnel today. The electricity had been turned off and the only illumination would come from the headlamps on the men's helmets.

Gordon was still reluctant to move.

"Can we not get to the other side any other way?"

"You got a boat?"

"You're a bunch o' sissies." Young Rab stepped forward. Youngest of the group. Still a teenager on his first job. "Nothing to be scared of in there."

He was bouncing from foot to foot.

"This is where I take my birds."

"Aye, but, how far do you go?" Gordon asked.

"As far as they'll let me."

That set them all laughing. Rab was new to the team but they liked him.

"You're no' gonnae let the boy go in by hisself, Gordon?" Willie said.

"Don't need anybody." Rab had already begun to head inside the tunnel. "At least I'll be out of the rain."

He switched on his helmet lamp and sent a ribbon of light into the darkness.

"Keeping shouting and letting us know you're okay."

Rab didn't even turn. "Why should I not be okay?"

"You've got to hand it to wee Rab." Rossi smiled. "Scared of nothing."

Rossi was the oldest of the team. Retiring in two weeks and it couldn't come fast enough.

"Still here!" Rab shouted, waving, smiling with a full set of bright white teeth.

They waved back. Gordon felt a bit silly now, watching the youngest of them going boldly where he had been wary of treading.

"Still here!" Rab called again. Now he was shrouded in darkness and it looked to Rossi as if it was hovering around, waiting for him. He shrugged away such a stupid idea.

Then Rab was gone.

"He'll be at the other side in five minutes." Willie checked his watch. "Knowing Rab he'll run."

But five minutes passed and there was no word from the boy. They called into the tunnel.

"Rab!"

No reply.

"He's winding us up." Gordon said.

"He should be out by now." The foremen checked his watch again. "I'll kill that boy."

"Maybe he's hurt," Rossi said. "He could have tripped or something."

"He's winding us up," Gordon repeated.

"Anybody got his number?" The foreman asked. But Rab was new. Why would any of them have his number?

"Me and Gordon, we'll go through and find him." Sharkey stepped forward. "I'll murder him myself if this is a piss take."

It was clear from the look on Gordon's face he still didn't want to go. But he wouldn't back down, now that young Rab had gone in so boldly.

"Aye fine."

Gordon and Sharkey switched on their headlamps and ventured in. Sharkey held up his phone.

"We'll keep in touch. I'll text you."

Rossi didn't take his eyes off the men till they too seemed to be swallowed by the darkness.

A few minutes later Willie held out his mobile so Rossi could see the message. "Sharkey's just texted. No sign of Rab."

And then they heard it, a low wail winding its way out of the passageway.

Willie dialled Sharkey's number and shouted into the phone.

"Sharkey! What's that?"

"We heard it as well!" On the other end, Sharkey sounded annoyed. "It's that bloody boy."

The phone went dead.

Willie kept trying to call but heard nothing else.

"What's going on in there?"

Minutes later, Sharkey emerged from the darkness.

"I cannae find Gordon noo. One minute he was right beside me, and then...he wasn't."

Sharkey was still standing in the tunnel mouth when another Sharkey, appeared on the opposite side of the canal. He, too, was waving and shouting.

"Cannae find him, Boss."

Both of them were yelling at the same time.

"Do you see what I see?" Willie's voice trembled.

He didn't need an answer. Rossi's face was white, his mouth open. Both Sharkey's called out again.

"What'll I do Boss?"

"Come back!" Willie answered, though he didn't know which man he was talking to.

The Sharkey on the bank waved and disappeared. The Sharkey in the tunnel bellowed. "I think I hear something."

Before they could stop him, he turned and sprinted back into the darkness. It looked to Rossi as if the dimness had come alive and followed the man in.

"Do you know something, Willie?" He turned to his foreman. "Something about this tunnel?"

"It was such a long time ago." Willie nodded his head. "I was only young myself when I was first sent in there. It had a leak and I was sealing up the roof. I'd see shadows out of the corner of my eye, but when I looked, there was nobody there. When I came back the boss said *Have you forgot something?*

I told him I had finished and he laughed.

Who are you trying to kid? You only went in there two minutes ago.

I tried to tell him I was there for hours, and he wouldn't believe me. And when I looked at my watch, he was right. I went in at nine o clock and came out before five past nine. Never came near the place again, till this morning."

He shuddered.

"Something happens when you're in there, Rossi. Something you just cannae explain."

He held out his mobile.

"Get the manager here, pronto. My hands are shaking too much."

Rossi's hands were trembling too. It took him a few minutes to send the text

They heard another cry.

"Help! Help me!" It was Sharkey's voice. "God's sake help me."

"We've got to go in," The foreman said.

"I'm not setting foot in there." Rossi was two weeks till his retirement. He was going on a cruise with his wife.

Another cry came out of the darkness, the moan of a soul in agony.

"Help, oh please God, help."

"We've got to." Willie straightened up. "Something's happened to our crew."

Rossi hesitated. Then it all fell into place.

This was a trick to wind him up, because he was leaving soon. They always tried a hoax with the old blokes before they retired. Aye, that was it. A hoax.

The thought made him feel better. Confident enough to head into the passage.

"C'mon then. Let's get this sorted."

It was only as they entered the mouth that his bravado failed. They couldn't hear the traffic on the nearby road, or the rain as it hammered through the trees. It was as if the world outside the tunnel didn't exist.

They called out for their mates but got no answer.

Rossi didn't want to lose sight of Willie and it seemed Willie felt the same. Would have held hands if it hadn't been so stupid.

But the passage seemed to go on forever.

Rossi shone his light around and suddenly, there was Rab. He was in a side tunnel, facing the wall.

"Rab!" Rossi shouted, puzzled. How could there be a side tunnel?

The boy turned his face, making the older man stop dead. There was something wrong with his eyes. Just red pinpoints in the blackness.

"Rossi! Where are ye?" Willie called. His voice seemed farther away than it ought to be.

"Wait there, Rab." Rossi hurried back and found Willie standing in the darkness.

"I saw Sharkey," the foreman said. "And then the blackness took him."

"What do you mean?" Rossi grabbed his arm. "The blackness took him?"

"It came from the roof." Willie pointed. Came down and swallowed him up. We've got to get out of here."

"No, come this way." Rossi tugged at him. "I found Rab!"

They ran together. Rossi wasn't sure he'd find the boy again but there he was, in the same place, staring at the wall.

"Come on Rab. We're getting out of here."

Rab looked round but didn't move

Willie let out a long moan.

"What's wrong with his eyes?"

"It's the beam of the torch making them look like that."

He made a move to pull away from Willie but the man held him fast.

"Leave him. We can send somebody in later."

"We can't just abandon the boy." Rossi tried again. "Rab come on!"

Why wouldn't he answer? Why wouldn't he move?

"It's the blackness, I'm telling you. It swallowed Sharkey." Willie was shaking with fear. "There's something in here with us."

He began to run back the way he had come.

Rossi hesitated. Then his nerve broke and he fled too. The men said nothing as they ran, trying to keep pace with each other. Rossi stumbled and went down hard, head cracking on the ground.

Willie hauled his companion to his feet.

"Come on!"

Rossi's chest grew tight and he began to wheeze. He had his inhaler in one of his pockets but dared not stop to find it. He wanted to live. He wanted to enjoy his retirement with his wife. He wanted to go on that cruise. He didn't even know what he was running from.

"Where the hell is the end of the tunnel?" Willie gasped.

They should be seeing the entrance by now. Why was it getting darker?

Then an oval of light at last. The mouth of the tunnel. Rossi put on a burst of speed and passed Willie.

"We're going to make it!"

The glow was so close he could reach out and touch it. He threw himself forward and landed on the muddy path. His fingers found the inhaler and he drew a deep breath from it.

Within seconds he could feel his own passageway clear and he looked back into the tunnel where Willie was still running frantically.

Why wasn't he out of there yet? He didn't seem to be moving forward. The foreman held out a pleading hand but darkness seemed to be wrapping itself around him.

Rossi watched through his fingers until all that was left of Willie were two red pinpoints of eyes and the sound of a scream fading into nothing. The mouth of the tunnel grew smaller and smaller, as if it were folding in on itself.

Then it was gone.

Rossi took a long pull on his inhaler again and put a hand to his head. He was bleeding from where he had fallen. He felt sick.

Where were Willie, and Rab and Gordon and Sharkey? Where were they?

A council lorry headed down the path towards him. Matt, the manager jumped from the passenger seat and crouched beside him.

"You okay, Rossi? Just stay still and get your breath back. You're bleeding."

Rossi pointed to where the tunnel used to be. "It's gone."

"What's gone?"

The tunnel. It's gone."

"I've no idea what you're talking about."

It took Rossi a moment to register what his boss had said.

"The tunnel we came to close up."

Matt shook his head.

"Rossi, I sent you here to check the canal level because of the rain."

"But we've got to find Willie and Rab and Sharkey and...the... other one."

"Willie *who*?"

"Willie Tosh. The foreman....and young Rab, they're in there."

"I sent you out on your own." Matt held a hankie against Rossi's bleeding head. "Looks like you've had a bad fall there. I think we should get you home."

Rossi wanted to go home, more than anything. But he had to help... Willie and... what was his name again? He felt he was letting someone down if he just left. There was something he had to do...what was it?

Maybe if he had a rest, it would all come back to him.

"Let's hear no more about these non-existent workmen and their tunnel, eh?" Matt helped him up. "You don't seem yourself, at all."

Rossi looked him in bewilderment.

"Tunnel?" he said. "What tunnel?"

Cathy Macphail has written dozens of books and is the winner of the Kathleen Fidler award

and the Scottish Children's Book Award (several times). Her young adult novel *Another Me* was recently turned into a movie. She also wrote two series of the BBC Radio sitcom *My Mammy and Me*.

What's the Story Morning Star Glory?

Gary Oberg

I know I am nothing special. I have not led an interesting life. But I have a secret I've never told anyone before.

When I was 13, I met the devil.

We played together in the Tamfourhill woods in the summer of 1983. I didn't know he was the devil. He said his name was Gilly. The thin, pale boy looked just like any other kid from the estate, except his irises were sky blue and artless as the glass eyes of my sister's dolls. The only thing diabolic about Gilly was his obsession with hurting insects but, in fairness, most of us kids pulled the wings of flies and ladybirds back then. We didn't have Iphones and You Tube videos to entertain our pubescent dark side.

I remember discussing the new boy with Andy and Sarah as we walked down the hill towards the woods.

"Naebody kens if he's even a Proddie or a Tim."

"Aye!" Andy agreed. "And he talks like some teuchtar fi *Take the High Road.*"

Sarah sighed in disgust. "Nane oh ye tubes had a mind to just ask him, eh?"

Her silhouette was black against the sinking white sun. She looked like the face on my mum's old cameo brooch.

"Boys!" Sarah rolled her eyes. "Well, I asked Gilly where he's fae. He tilled me he comes fi doon Sooth, but his folks travel aboot a lot so he gets taught at hame."

Sarah talked tough, as always, but she gently pressed my hand when Andy ran ahead into the woods.

Gilly was waiting for us by the big oak tree that day, that last summer day. Lee Major's face glowered on his Fall Guy t-shirt, but Gilly was all smiles.

"Hey Zeke," he beckoned to me. "Come and see this beehive I've set on fire. Does it smell like candle wax to you, altar boy?"

Yeah, Gilly liked setting fires but we all did back then. I carried matches myself, to melt plastic soldiers and the like. As I said, it was the eighties. The other kids checked out the melting beehive but I'm allergic to stings. Gilly had found some porn mags with the pages stuck together, but I didn't look at them either. I couldn't look at them with Sarah there, watching the flames.

"Well, Strength of God," Gilly liked to call me that. When we first met he told me it's what my name means in Hebrew. "What do you want to do, Ezekiel?"

"I'm naw wanting to see yer scuddie mags." I didn't like it when he used my proper name. "An I told you, I could snuff it if I get stung by a bee."

"I'm not asking you what you want to do right now. What do you want to do after you finish school?"

"I want to be an author." I told him. "Not kiddie stuff like aw that Famous Five, Hardy Boys and Nancy Drew bollocks, mind. I want to make up great stories, like Stephen King."

"You don't want to write just for fame and fortune, then?"

"Naw, I'm no like yon Jackie Collins or Danielle Steel that ma maw likes!" I could not lie to my inquisitive friend's blue eyes. "I want to write aboot things that really matter, ken? I want to move people. I want to make them feel more than any other writer has ever done before."

Gilly turned away from me then and we sat in silence and watched the other kids burning the porn mags. I worried that the sly boy would tell all my friends about my secret ambition. I was frightened they would mock me for not being lowly wise. No great writer had ever come from Tamfourhill.

Then Gilly nudged me. "Come on."

He took me back to the oak tree and he told me to close my eyes. I hesitated, but then I squeezed my lids shut and held my breath. Nothing happened for a moment, and then suddenly I felt a tugging at my chest as if someone was pulling at my polo shirt.

"Look and see!"

I looked. The boy was holding a big butterfly with iridescent blue and pink wings in his cupped hands. It was beautiful.

"Pull its wings off."

"What?

"Pull its wings off and your wish will come true." His smile vanished. "Your words will have such power, Strength of God."

I reached out with shaking hands to the butterfly. I breathed hard on its wings, willing it to take off, but it did not move. It could have been made of plastic. I told myself that it was. I took the butterfly wings in my trembling fingers and I pulled them both at the same time. One little tug and it was done. Strength of God indeed!

Gilly snatched the crushed wings from my stained fingers and he burnt them with his Zippo lighter. It was all over so quickly. I didn't even see the body of the poor creature fall.

"Is that it?" I didn't feel any different.

"It is done." Gilly flicked his wrist and the lighter snapped shut. "Go home and write something. Anything at all, Zeke. I'll meet you back here tonight.

Bring your friend and your girlfriend too. We will be your first fans."

I went home and got a jotter from my school bag. I couldn't think of anything original to write so I did what any schoolboy would do. I used the last thing I'd seen. It was a Stephen King film about a rabid dog called Cujo. I don't even remember what I called the dog in my story, but I recall my tale began with some boys playing in the woods. One of the boys, a nasty bully, stones a beehive - even though the hero, a boy called Zack, is allergic to bee stings. The angry insects attack and the kids run, but the allergic boy trips and falls.

Zack's big, black Alsatian dog crouches over its master to protect him from the bees and they sting it instead, until it goes nuts with the pain. The dog turns on the other kids and tears the nasty boy apart. The crazed beast goes to attack its master but then, at the last moment, it dives wide and lands head first in the hive. The dog's head is stuck and the bees sting and sting the poor animal as it roars and whimpers in pain.

In the end Zack picks up the brick and, crying as the bees sting him, he smashes the beehive and the skull of his dog.

My story certainly wasn't original and I didn't know if it was any good. I felt nervous as I crouched in the dark, on the roots of the big oak with my friends. They all sat in silence while I read out my shaggy dog story. I didn't look up at them until I was finished.

"So!" I stared at their blank faces. "What do you think?"

There was a pause until Gilly clapped warmly. It was a good start!

Then Sarah covered her mouth with her hands and let out a despairing wail. Andy tilted his head back and laughed and laughed. I had hoped for some kind of reaction and I had got three very different results from my test audience. I watched them with bemused interest at first, but my friends just carried on clapping, screaming and laughing.

Sarah was hysterical. Tears flowed from her eyes and her scalp bled as she plucked locks of her blonde hair out by the roots. Andy fell on the ground and rolled there, tears streaming down his cheeks.

"It stuck," he giggled. "It stuck on Moj. On Mo! Mm!"

The words caught in Andy's throat, his face flushed red and then he began to spasm and writhe. I rushed to my stricken friend but didn't know what to do.

"Gilly!" I cried. "He's choking, help me!"

I looked for the other boy, but he was gone.

I never saw him again.

Andy's eyes rolled back into his head. He convulsed and twitched and then he stopped moving.

Sarah still sat there clutching her head, screaming and screaming.

I turned then and ran. I guess, in a way, I've never stopped.

I told everyone that I had found Andy lying dead and Sarah hysterical and I had no idea what had really happened to them. I told the police that Gilly was there too but they never found him.

You might have heard about this tragedy before. It made the national news at the time. I am the unnamed boy who helped the police with their enquiries. The cops found burnt porn mags and an empty U-hu glue tub near the tree, so television and newspaper journalists moralised about the dangers of adolescent obsessions with pornography, pyromania and drugs.

Self-abuse and solvent abuse, huh? Lazy fucking hacks! None of them were real writers. They had no integrity or imagination.

Andy and Sarah's parents suspected that I knew more than I let on, but I couldn't admit what really happened. Couldn't risk telling a story again, even a true one. So, I've never spoken of what happened in the woods that day. Until now.

I struck a match and torched my cursed tale. As I watched it burn, like those butterfly wings, I realised my only choices were to either play dumb or be honest about everything from then on. No more paltry lies or stories for the Strength of God. I learned to tell the absolute truth.

Try and imagine how incredibly difficult it would be for a teenager not to tell a story or sell a lie. That was my life.

Being earnest and honest all the time was agony for a would-be tale-spinner, but this was my penance. And, after several years of silence and solitude, it became almost natural for me.

Almost.

I have never had any other friends or girlfriends since that day and most of my colleagues at the call centre see me as a humourless bore. There are a few self-obsessed idiots in the office who like to tell me about their tedious lives, as they think my silence means I am a good listener. They'll never know how much I scream inside, desperately wanting to tell them to shut the fuck up. I don't want to listen. I want to talk and joke and curse, like everyone else. I want to exaggerate and amaze and be the centre of attention while others hang on my every word.

Some nights I dream about the doll-eyed boy and, in my dreams, I beg.

"Please Gilly." I clutch at his cupped palms. "Please give me back my butterfly."

Gilly just smiles and claps his empty hands at my performance.

Sometimes, when I am alone in my little flat, I write stories in dusty journals. I rattle out random tales about real and imaginary people and places, but I never know if they are any good, not without an audience. I just burn them when I'm done. I use a gun-metal Zippo lighter instead of matches now. The lighter has a grinning red devil head on it. I reckon Andy would have approved of that little joke.

I only speak to one person. Sarah's folks are long gone but their estate still pays for her sanatorium sanctuary. I often sit with her in her room, or on a bench in the gardens, and tell her about my boring life while she rocks back and forward and cries.

I like to squeeze her hand and tell her: *You were my first and only love.*

Sarah has only a few straw white hairs left on her scalp now. She has wept for so long, she's worn two vertical channels into sunken cheeks, below her streaming red eyes. Still, sometimes when I squint at her profile in the sinking sun, I get a glimpse of the young girl who once walked beside me into the woods.

"I am so sorry Sarah." I told her on my last visit. "So, so sorry."

"Poor Mojo," she sobbed in response. "Poor, poor Mojo!"

There are times when I convince myself that none of this is my fault. There are the dark, brooding nights when my paranoia makes me doubt everything I saw and heard on that terrible day. What if Gilly told Andy and Sarah about my literary pretensions and they decided to play a prank on me, to ridicule my lofty aspirations? Perhaps my friends only pretended to be moved by my silly story. Maybe they planned their performance in advance but the scheme went awry. Maybe Andy choked while he was mocking me, and this caused Sarah to have some kind of hysterical reaction. Then the ringleader Gilly took off, so he didn't get the blame. That's why I ran away after all.

The strange little home-schooled boy probably moved on with his rich family after the summer, while I was left here alone, self-punished and unpublished, forever.

I don't really know what happened back then, but I guess I have reached a place in my pointless, wasted life where I have to know the truth, no matter what the consequences.

It is possible I have ruined my life over a childish joke and that notion is unbearable to me.

That's why I went back to Tamfourhill last night for the first time in thirty-four years.

The woods had been replaced by an industrial estate, but one defiant oak tree still stood, next to a shut down burger van and locked-up garage. I brought a journal and, as the sun set, I sat against the tree and wrote this. The confession of a justified sinner.

Like I said, I'm nothing special. We all tell stories. We exaggerate, gossip, and lie. It doesn't matter really if we talk just to entertain and impress, or to imprint our ideals on others. Words have power. Everyone wants to be the centre of attention; even if just for a few precious seconds. A captive audience validates the storyteller's existence.

I have fought my nature for 35 years, but what I said to Gilly, back then in the woods, remains true to this day. I want to make people feel, something, anything. I want to make them feel more than any other writer has ever done before.

I am almost finished. We will soon see if there really is any power in my words. Dear reader; faithful listener, I will sit and wait anxiously while you decide the end of my tale. This confession may have meant everything or nothing at all.

Yes, I will wait.

And we will discover together if this is a story about a boy who made a deal with the devil, or a tale told by an idiot, who was once tricked by a sick little bastard who liked to pluck the wings off butterflies.

Gary Oberg is 48. A writer from Falkirk and, regular contributor at *Wooer with Words*, he has had stories published in *#Untitled Magazine* and *Alight Here: An Anthology of Falkirk Writing*. His story *Pramface-Off* won the Falkirk Libraries Writing Rammy competition and he is currently editing his first novel *Down Bromian Way*. When not working and writing, he can usually be found staggering around the streets of Grangemouth in an increasingly futile attempt to keep fit.

There's Something Wrong with the Baby

Samantha Maclaren

The nosebleeds began in the summer, the year after Tess lost the baby.

The night was very hot. She lay on top of the duvet, body curled towards the space where Oliver usually slept, as had Tom before him. In the quiet dark, she dreamt of the man she loved, as the first trickle of dark blood ran down her cheek and hit the pillow.

Tess spluttered into wakefulness, a dirty metal taste in her mouth. One foot still planted in sleep, her first thought was disjointed—her wisdom teeth removed at nineteen; she vomited watery blood all over the backseat of her father's car on the drive home. No pain, only the expectation of it as the anesthetic wore off. No pain now. Only a thick pulsing sensation up high in her nose, near the eye.

The trickle became a steady stream. Tess stumbled from the bed, slick hand sliding across the bathroom

63

tiles as she groped for the light switch. She hunched over the sink, breathing wetly, watching the fat, dark drops splatter the porcelain with alarming speed.

A scream was perched at the back of her throat. She imagined the basin filling and filling until it overflowed with the vile stuff, dripping down her thighs, splashing her bare feet. She closed her eyes until the flow trickled to nothing, trying not to cry.

Her legs were shaking.

Turning on the cold tap, she watched the pink water wash itself clear. Her hands were smeared red, right up her wrists, over the scars. How much they had bled, when she opened herself up and poured out her life, drop by drop, into the bathtub. One hand was hanging over the rim when Tom found her, bright red and dripping. Tess thought about it every day, it was impossible not to. But usually she dwelt only on the enclosing darkness, the swallowing horror of what had happened, or failed to happen. Now, here was the blood again. She couldn't take her eyes off it.

With a gasp, she plunged both hands under the stream of water. She was struck by the terrible idea that they could not be cleaned, that they would come out redder than ever.

But that was foolish. She'd had a little fright was all. She dampened a facecloth and wiped the smears from her cheek, her chin, dabbed at the nostril, tilted her face to the tap and rinsed her mouth out. Then she returned to bed.

The sheets and pillow case were spattered with it. She would need to scrub drops off the carpet in the morning. Tess stripped off her bloody nightdress and climbed, naked, into the clean side of the bed. Once it was Tom's side. Now Oliver's. She wanted to phone him but she wouldn't. How silly she would feel, to wake him over a bad nosebleed. And she would see him tomorrow. Oliver. Her Oliver. Not Tom.

Her scars itched. It took a long time for sleep to find her again.

"I'm sorry I wasn't there."

"Oh, no. I'm glad you weren't; it was *not* a pretty sight. Think Carrie on prom night."

He smiled his soft smile. Tess found herself smiling, too. She seemed to be doing a lot of that lately. If someone had told her this a year ago, after the baby and Tom. The bathtub. She would have laughed until she wept. But here she was. Smiling, and eating pancakes.

Sitting by the window with the warm sunlight on her face and Oliver across the table, she could not remember why she'd been so upset the previous night. It was a trigger, she thought, recalling one of the stock phrases so often wheeled out in her support group. She hadn't seen that much blood since...

Don't fucking dwell on it. It's over.

"How long did it last?" Oliver said, around a mouthful of bread.

"Five minutes, maybe. I wasn't exactly timing it."

"I don't think it's serious unless it lasts longer than a half hour."

"I know. It just gave me a bit of a fright."

"Of course it did," he said. He began to cut up his breakfast again, then put down his fork. He fixed her with a look she recognised, another staple of the support group where they'd met.

"How are you feeling today?"

She glanced across the quiet café. Other couples. A family with a gurgling infant smearing jam on its face. Two waitresses peering through the service hatch, laughing at something in the kitchen. Oliver, eating French toast.

"I'm feeling a whole lot better," she said.

He reached across the table and squeezed her hand. Tess could not comprehend his strength and optimism. Most of the survivors in the support group, herself included, were fragile as broken teacups held together with Prozac.

She didn't know what Oliver's trauma was. He wasn't a big sharer, even in group, and didn't have any visible scars. Pills, maybe. It didn't matter. He was a fighter, and he would fight for her too. He wouldn't let her slip into the darkness, like Tom had.

That was too kind. Tom had seen her sliding and pushed.

She resisted the urge to tell Oliver she loved him. It was too soon. And maybe it didn't need to be said.

"I feel safe with you," she said instead.

He turned his face away. She thought maybe he was trying not to cry.

The second nosebleed came less than a week later, while Tess was at work. Her nasal passage had felt stuffed up all week and there was that pulsing sensation again, that odd wriggling thickness. Then the first drop hit her keyboard with a delicate plop.

The men at the surrounding desks all looked up, like dogs scenting the first blood of a hunt. Two more drops fell, then it began to gush.

"Christ, not again," Tess muttered, cupping her hands under her nose and power walking in the direction of the bathroom.

In a show of solidarity or morbid curiosity, two female colleagues followed her in and chattered uneasily across her head, while Tess hunched over the sinks and waited for it to stop. They never knew what to say to her since her return to work.

Both were still married. Alice's daughter was starting school in August. Rebecca had a three-year-old and another on the way. Tess remembered, faintly, how special and right it had felt to be a part of that club. How the girls in the office had squealed when she showed them Tom's ring; how they had cooed over her swelling belly. These were the women who would all be on the PTA together; the women who made granola bars for the church bake sale; who were politely concerned about Muslims, homosexuals and gluten. Women who gossiped about the other office girls (look at Gina's tattoos, she'll never find a man looking like that and hasn't Elsa gained weight) behind manicured hands with false glittering smiles. Who sent flowers to the hospital when their friend lost her child and husband and tried to take her own life.

But they didn't visit.

How very nice it had been, part of that narrow little world. Her mother would have approved.

"You've got some on your blouse." Alice sounded clipped and proper, not at all like she had when confiding in Tess that she liked her husband to tie her to the bed frame with one of his many paisley silk ties. "Do you have anything else to wear?"

"I've got a cardigan at my desk," Tess said. "I'll just put it on over."

She did not fail to notice the way their eyes dropped at once to her scars as she scrubbed the blood from her hands, nor the look they shot one another. They would probably talk about her later over non-fat lattes. Wasn't it terrible what that poor girl did to herself, no wonder he left her, she must be mad, that's probably how she lost the baby in the first place. She couldn't stand their greedy eyes on her personal tragedy and asked if they'd give her a minute alone.

Rebecca put a tentative hand on her shoulder.

"We're always here if you want to talk, Tess. And Jonathan and I would love to have you over for dinner sometime."

They left and Tess felt dreadful. She thought the whole world was out to get her these days. She wept in one of the cubicles, then put herself back together and returned to her desk, as though nothing had happened.

Three more nosebleeds within as many days and Tess took herself to the hospital to get checked out. The doctor assured her it would be nothing serious as he tilted her head back to take a look. Probably a weak blood vessel and was she taking any medication which might be thinning her blood? People came in every day believing their brain was bleeding out their nose and it never was. Almost. More often than not...

He froze, his face almost comical in its surprise.

"What is it?" Tess asked, breathless. "Is it serious?"

"Uh... I don't want to alarm you..." The doctor cleared his throat. In that moment, Tess imagined a hundred terrible ways she might be dying.

"What?"

"Um... There's a large leech in your nasal passage."

She had prepared herself for a brain tumour and was still shocked into silence. She listened without hearing as he explained how he was going to remove the thing. Tried to ignore the cluster of curious medical staff who gathered to watch as the doctor laid her on the table. She closed her eyes and tried not to think about the last time she'd been in this hospital, with ugly black stitches in her wrists, or the time before that, when she finally went into labour, and the pushing was done. Tom's sombre words of comfort had trickled to a speechless end and that terrible dead thing which should have been a baby girl finally slid out of her in a wash of blood. As she felt it leave she'd broken down at last and screamed until they put her under. That awful interior pulling, that wet, sliding sensation as the doctor pulled the thing out of her.

Tess bit down on her lip until it bled. She wanted to scream and scream.

"Teresa? It's out."

It's a girl.

Tess opened her eyes. Her nose was trickling, but that thick wet feeling was gone.

The doctor was holding up a plastic tube, and Tess might have mistaken the object inside it for a blood clot, except it was moving. Pulsing. It was almost as big as her thumb.

"That… was inside me?"

The doctor held the tube up to his eye. "To be honest, I've never seen anything like it, not in this country. It's unpleasant, but there's no long-term damage. How long did you say you'd been experiencing bleeding?"

"Over a week."

The thing in the tube shifted, leaving a red smear on the plastic.

"It must have gorged itself," the doctor murmured.

Tess looked away, nauseated. "How did it get there?"

"Well, that's the prize-winning question, isn't it? Have you visited a foreign country recently?"

"I haven't travelled in years."

"Hmm. Been swimming in any rivers or lakes?"

"No."

The doctor shrugged. "It's a mystery. The important thing is, it's out. Do you want to keep it?"

She was revolted. The doctor took it away and left it on his desk until it died, three days later.

"Poor thing," Oliver murmured, kissing her neck from behind as she sat at her computer. "Are you okay?"

Tess hesitated. She didn't feel okay.

"It was a shock."

He put his arms around her. She shrugged him off, with a difficult smile.

"I've got work to do, darling."

Oliver kissed the top of her head then left her to it. He returned later with ice-cream and sat cross-legged on the couch beside her while they ate. They talked in the way Tess had never been able to with Tom, whose eyes had wandered to the television, or the newspaper, or another woman as she spoke. Tess realized she'd always accepted that as just part of the package when it came to men, along with leaving the toilet seat up and never cleaning the sink after shaving. All the men in her life had been the same, right back to her father. Until Oliver.

Oliver was unlike any of her previous lovers. That surprise had excited and scared Tess in equal measure. He was very much like a woman, she often thought—had a certain delicacy about him, an unconscious grace. He reminded her of the girls she'd loved in college, before Tom came along and old friendships died outside of the dozy cocoon that was married life. Oliver seemed genuinely invested in her happiness and well-being.

"What happened to the, um, the leech?" he asked, suddenly.

Tess swallowed. "I don't know. The doctor took it away."

"Poor thing."

"Me or the leech?"

He smiled, but it didn't seem to sit right on his face.

"Well, it didn't know any better."

"Still a vile parasite," Tess muttered, rubbing the back of her neck. "Speaking of which, I think something bit me. This spot's been itchy and sore for days."

"I can kiss it better…"

His lips did not linger on her neck long, but were soon moving down her throat, her chest. Fingers fumbled with the buttons on her blouse. One pale breast free, his mouth over her nipple, gently teasing... Tess stifled a moan, and pushed his head away.

"I've still got work to do. Maybe later."

"It's late," Oliver murmured, one hand on her thigh, slipping under her skirt. "Come to bed and I'll make you forget..."

"Mmmm, no. My boss will be the one making me bleed if I don't get this report finished for tomorrow."

"Screw your boss. Come to bed and quit your job tomorrow. I know you hate it."

"And do what instead?"

He kissed his way up the inside of her thigh. "Stay in bed all day with me, and paint at night. I'll let you paint me."

"How did you know I used to paint?"

"Hmm?"

"How did you know I used to paint? I never told you that."

"I found your stash of half-finished canvases. Very beautiful. Come to bed."

She shoved him away this time, pulling her blouse closed over her chest.

"My canvases are in the nursery."

"What?"

"My canvases are all stored in the nursery. I don't go in the nursery. You know that. Why were you in the nursery?"

He saw the hurt etched deep in the lines on her face. He lowered his head.

"I'm sorry. I didn't realise which room it was. The door was unmarked and wasn't locked."

Tess removed her reading glasses, rubbed her eyes. "You must have had a pretty good look though, if you saw the pictures. They're at the back, beside the crib. Under a sheet."

Oliver said nothing.

"I did most of those while I was pregnant," Tess murmured, almost to herself. Without realising it, her hand came to rest on her belly. "Tom travelled a lot for work in those days. I would paint in secret while he was away. I wanted to surprise him."

Her voice caught in her throat; it took her a moment to continue. Both hands cradled her flat stomach now.

"They were for the baby's room. So she... it would grow up surrounded by its mother's loving work." Her voice had dropped to little more than a whisper.

"I loved my creations so much, even before they were finished."

Tears were rolling down her cheeks. She didn't notice. She was reliving that last fight, in the nursery she and Tom had painted together, beside the crib that would never be used. He had been angry that she refused to name the baby, that she insisted they cremated it. He hadn't understood the horror she would have felt in knowing that terrible wet thing was rotting in a silk-lined coffin as it had in her womb. He hadn't had to carry it around inside himself, what should have been his baby. Hadn't had to birth it, knowing it was already dead. He left her because she was selfish. Because she didn't understand. He wanted a family, he deserved a family, after what he'd been through. She could no longer conceive.

He left and did not call. He returned to the house only once, after filing for divorce. Returned to pick up his belongings and found Tess bleeding out in the bathtub.

There was a pregnant silence.

"I'm really sorry I brought it up," Oliver said, quietly. "I didn't realise you'd painted them during your pregnancy. I thought the fumes would have been dangerous for the baby."

Tess closed her eyes, her lip trembling. "You sound just like Tom."

They went to bed but did not have sex. Tess lay awake for hours, scratching her scars. When she managed to sleep, she dreamt of Tom, of his new wife. Their little girl.

In the small hours, she woke to find leeches crawling on her legs.

Screaming, she scrambled across the bed and toppled over the edge, smacking her head on the side table as she went down.

She blacked out.

She was sprawled on the floor in a tangled heap of sheets and limbs. Oliver was over her, his hand in her hair and his face twisted in concern.

The memory came back to her like a punch to the gut. Tess jerked and began to swipe at her flesh, crying, begging him to get them off her, get them off.

"Tess! Tess, calm down. You've had some kind of episode, but you're safe. You're safe. I'm here."

"There's leeches!" Tess screamed, ripping the sheets as she tried to free herself, clawing at her legs. "Get them off me!"

Oliver grabbed her wrists and held them still. "Tess, look at me. You had a nightmare. There was a leech in your nose but it's gone."

"No. No... They were here, they were on me, in the bed," Tess moaned, struggling weakly against him. "Look."

She glanced at her legs.

"No leeches," Oliver said, softly. "No blood. You had a nightmare."

"But... But I felt them," Tess whispered, hearing the shake in her voice. "They... I..."

"It's over," Oliver murmured, stroking her hair. "Come back to bed."

She folded into his arms like a child and wept herself into silence. When she was finished, he carried her to the bed. She checked the sheets again. Nothing there. Oliver watched but didn't say anything. When she lay down, he pulled her close.

"I'm not crazy," she whispered.

"I'm sure you're not," Oliver said, sounding very sad.

A week passed. The nosebleeds stopped, but the bite on Tess's neck was joined by others on her stomach and hands, her ankles, even the backs of her knees. Oliver suggested it might be bed bugs. They stripped the mattress and washed the sheets.

The nightmares continued. Tess found she could no longer sleep without Oliver's arms around her. All the progress she'd made in the support group had been undone. She felt as though her sutures had been ripped open, and she was bleeding freely.

She was also becoming anaemic. At least, she thought she was, pale and light-headed and felt exhausted all the time. But she couldn't bring herself to go back to the hospital and find out. Oliver brought her iron supplements and petted her hair. Told her to get some rest.

She took time off work. She couldn't stand to look at the other women anymore, with their happy marriages and their beautiful, healthy children. She stayed home and avoided the nursery. Avoided the crib as it gathered dust.

She wished she'd sold the house and relocated, when she possessed the energy. Tom had the right idea. He'd moved on to greener pastures. One morning while Oliver was out, Tess had driven to Tom's new house in the suburbs and watched from her car for over an hour. His new wife was very pretty.

Oliver was acting strange, or maybe he wasn't. He seemed distant, or perhaps she was paranoid. Tess couldn't tell the difference anymore. Her mind was a writhing pit of snakes. He whispered comforting things and held her at night when the nightmares gripped her, but his heart didn't seem to be in it. Perhaps he would leave her too.

Everybody did, in the end.

The night was very hot.

In the quiet dark, Tess dreamt of the man she loved, as the first trickle of dark blood leaked from between her legs.

She woke first to wetness, then to a dreadful wriggling between her thighs.

"Tom," she gasped, hoarse with panic, reaching out for him. "Tom, I think something's wrong with the baby!"

But Tom wasn't there. Tom was asleep in his own bed very far from here, beside his beautiful, fertile new wife. Oblivious, as he'd always been.

Oliver sat on the edge of the bed, his back to her. He wasn't moving. Tess blinked at him, confused, before that wet, wriggling feeling came again. She screamed, convulsing as if in labour. The baby was gone, the baby was dead, but there was something there. Oh God, there was something inside her now.

"Help me!" she cried, grasping Oliver's arm and shaking him. "Oliver, help me, please. I'm bleeding!"

At first, Oliver didn't react. Then, very slowly, he turned to face her.

In the darkness of the room, it took Tess a moment to realize what was wrong. Oliver's eyes had rolled back in his skull like he was having a seizure. His jaw hung open, too wide, as though unhinged. And there was something wrong with his tongue. It looked too big for his mouth, too thick. And it was moving. Pulsing.

She realised that the thing in Oliver's mouth was a leech pulling itself free over his lip, another rising from his throat.

Tess began to scream. Then the thing inside her bit down, and the world swam away.

She was in the bathtub.

Tess raised her head a fraction, woozy. Saw the blood beginning to well again from her wrists, running down the porcelain in rivulets.

Oliver knelt beside the tub, holding a razorblade. A leech was crawling out of his eye socket, lower lid bulging as it pulled itself free. With his free hand, he reached up and prised it out, careful not to squash the fat little body. He kissed it.

Tess began to cry, out of fear or misery, she didn't know which. It didn't seem to matter.

"I'm sorry, Tess," Oliver said, but he didn't sound like Oliver anymore, not really. There was something in his voice Tess hadn't heard before. Or maybe she just hadn't wanted to.

"I didn't want to hurt you. I liked you." He set the leech down on the side of the tub, beside her open wrist. "I kept you alive longer than most, only letting them take a little. Amounts that you could survive. But the children… Well, they get so hungry."

Tess saw them then, dozens and dozens of them on the floor tiles, squirming up the sides of the tub. Some were almost as thick as her wrist. Oliver's eyes took them all in, brimming with hideous affection.

"What are you?" Tess whimpered. She tried to lift her wrists, to stop this, but was now too weak to do anything at all.

"A mother," Oliver said, placidly. "I don't like to hurt people. I only let my children feed on those who want to die. That's how I met you, at the support group. I didn't want to let them take you. But the poor things were starving to death."

The leeches bristled on the rim of the tub. Oliver smiled affectionately down at them.

Tess could barely see through tears in her eyes.

"I loved you," she whispered. "And you're just... just a parasite. Just like he was. Like they all are."

"Love is parasitic," Oliver said. "All women exist to be fed on. You love your child and you bleed for it, and it feeds off you forever. But a mother endures. You understand. You were almost one once."

"I... I killed my child," Tess said, feeling the dark tide of unconsciousness begin to lap at her mind. She remembered it well. She would tread water until her wrists ran dry, and then go under, and be lost.

"I didn't know... I didn't mean to do it... The paint..."

"It's okay," Oliver murmured, stroking her hair with his thumb. "You can be a mother now. Let the children feed."

As the leeches writhed over her gaping wrists, sucking and biting, Tess's eyes drifted closed. A smile settled over her lips. She dreamt of her child at her breast, as she followed it into the fathomless dark.

When it was done and the children were fat and fed, the thing that was Oliver stood and licked Tess's blood from both hands, a look of absent reflection on its borrowed face. It looked at her a minute more as the last of its offspring slipped back into their hiding places, then shook off its regret and headed for the door. A pamphlet for another support group, another town, was folded neatly in its pocket.

There was work to be done.

The children would not stay full for very long.

"Sammy" McLaren is a Scottish writer, artist, horror fanatic and staff writer at *Belladonna Horror Magazine*, the first horror magazine written and run entirely by women. Her articles have also appeared in prominent publications including *Paste Magazine*, *SciFiNow*, and *Scream the Horror Magazine*. In 2010, she won the Scottish Book Trust's Young Writers Award, and the following year was short listed for the Glass Woman Prize's Ghost Story Prize.

She currently lives in New York City.

Silence

David Macphail

Ah wakes up one day an everybody's gone. Not just ma girlfriend. She'd been lyin right nixt tae me. Or ma flatmate Stevie and his burd, who were in the flat. Ah mean everybody.

Ma family. Ma mates. Neighbours. Everybody in the street. Everybody in the toon. And their families, their friends. Their brurrs and sisters in the city. Their sons and daughters oot workin, or at college. Their great fuckin aunties livin in Millport. Their long lost relatives in Australia. The whole fuckin country. The whole fuckin world.

Fuck knows whit happened. They aw jist fucked off.

Course, ah don't realise that at first. Ah stretch oot ma arm, ah see she isnae there and reckon she's just got up early. It's a bit funny, she likes a lie-in on Saturdees, but whit else am ah tae think?

Yawn.

Ah rolls oot o' bed. Got a drouth and a sore heid fae the wine I drunk the night before. Ah wanders along the hall.

"Kellie? Kellie?"

Silence.

Ah think, she must have gone oot for rolls or sumhin. Ah makes maself a coffee, then sits doon tae watch tellie an huv a fag.

White noise.

"Ach! Whit?" Ah flicks through the channels. "Tch." Mer white noise.

Flick. Sigh.

"Ach." Flick.

"Och, come on, fur SUFFERING FUCK!"

Ah gets up and hits the TV a couple o times.

"Fuckin knew ah shouldnae've installed this fuckin box thing."

Mair white noise.

"Uh." Ah switches the TV back off. Wanders back intae the kitchen and puts on the radio.

Static.

"Uch, what the F…!" Ah switches it fae channel tae channel, but it's the same thing every time.

"Get digital they fuckin said."

Right then, ah still don't twig anythin's really wrong. Ah jist finish ma coffee and goes fur a shower.

It's no til efter ah come back intae the livin room that ah starts tae get worried. Ah tries her mobile.

Then ah hear it ringin. It's still in the hoose. In fact it's still in her bag.

Why wid she huv gone oot, ah mean, withoot her bag? She never goes anywhere withoot her bag.

Ah knocks on Steve's door. There's nae answer, so ah pushes it open. Steve's no there either. His bed's unmade, his curtains shut. He's fucked off as well.

Ah picks up her mobile and phones her Mum, thinkin she might huv gone there. Maybe mah snorin woke her up. Maybe she couldnae sleep.

There's nae answer. Ah tries her Dad's phone.

Rings oot. Same with her best pal, Evie.

Ah checks the front door. It's still locked and the chain's still on. If she'd gone oot then the chain wouldnae still be on, would it?

Right, this is gettin weird. Ah flings open the front door into the landing. Ah goes doon tae the front door and opens it.

It's foggy. Thae tendrils o cold mist ye get sometimes, they swirl roon the branches o the trees. There's naebody aboot. Naebody. And there's somethin weird. A difference. It takes me a bit o time tae work oot what it is.

Silence.

The kind a silence ye only really get in the country, climbin a munro or sumhin, sittin in a field looking over a glen or a loch. The kind o silence that's missin the background hum of human life. The rumble o traffic in the distance. The footsteps. Voices. TV sets blarin fae the flat windees. Instead ah kin hear pigeons roostin in the trees in the park, and the rush o the water over the weir, which you kin almost never hear durin the day.

Ah steps ontae the road. It's a quiet neighbourhood, a cul-de-sac that disnae see much traffic, but no this quiet. On a Saturday as well.

This is beginnin tae feel lit some fuckoff nightmare.

Is it somethin like curiosity, or maybe fear, that pulls me oan? Ah walks tae the end o the street. Fae there, it's no far tae the high street.

The high street's usually busy oan a Saturday, lined wi banks, shops, and cafés, but today the only things moving are seagulls. The shops are aw shut. There's naebody. Not a soul.

Ah walks aboot, searchin for somebody, anybody. Ah goes tae Tesco, but it's shut as well.

"HULLO! HULLO!"

There's no panic, jist shock. What's goin on? Is this some kinna big practical joke? Somethin that everybudy in the toon's in on except me?

Ah stands at the cross, that's normally buzzin wi traffic. Ah wait there fur a car. One car. A single truck. A lone biker. Anybudy that can set my mind at rest.

Five minutes is enough. Nae rider, nae truck or car is ever goin tae come.

Maybe there wus an evacuation that ah missed. A natural disaster? A gas leak? Fuckin Faslane going up?

Ah goes back to the flat. Ah calls my Mum. Five rings later ah get her call minder. Ma mate Burnie's phone's the same. An every other contact on ma mobile. Ah checks Steve's room again. His stuff's still there, his wallet, everythin.

Then the power goes off. The phones die. The TV. The toaster, the kettle, the lights.

"Fuck."

Ah opens a can o beans and eats them cold. Then ah walks. Walks aw the way intae the city proper. Doon to the Clyde, the river still flowin, but aw the people gone. Ah leans over the barriers, starin at the water.

My mind starts thinkin through aw the things ah need tae do now. Whit, pan the window in at Tesco, stock up on food an drink? Break intae Tisos and get my hands on a campin stove and some gas. Then, fuck knows. Smash intae the library, see if they've got a copy o the SAS survival handbook?

The power's gone. Everybody's gone. Have got tae go back to nature, raise livestock, set up greenhouses and grow ma own food, and that sort o shite. Ah'll huv to learn how to do everything maself, from pullin oot mah teeth, to operatin on mah own appendix, tae milkin cows.

It's like the start of some kin o post-apocalyptic Walkin Dead shite.

Then ah think, fuck that. Who am ah kidding? Ah work in a fuckin office, Ah'm stuck without a microwave, and ah've never been near a cow in aw my life. That's not me. This is desperate.

But that's not what does it. It's the silence.

Huv ye ever thought about how fuckin terrifying silence is? Real silence. It's inescapable. It surrounds ye. Sauchiehall Street. Argyll Street. Buchanan Street. Fucking silent.

Silent forever. Silent as the fuckin grave.

It's the baws.

Ah suck on another fag for a bit. My last one, before ah swing my legs over the railings and jump.

Silence.

David Macphail is the author of the children's book series *Thorfinn the Nicest Viking* and *Top-Secret Granddad and Me*. He has been short-listed for many prizes, including the LOLLIES, the Greenhouse Funny Prize and the Times/Chicken House Prize.

.

The Tenant

Anita Sullivan

They're all sleeping. Five students, four beds on the top floor of a sand-and-grime tenement. Above them, dead TV aerials and cold stars. Below, four floors of hidden lives descend with the shit-pipes and electric channels, down to the dirt of the long dead. Deacons, drunks, monks and resurrectionists, bone-shuffled together in obscurity.

The living are dreaming. Next to the kitchen, Flo and Gabrielle in single beds share a dream of unspoken love. In the neighbouring room, Rory's mind is a pink cave emptied by sex. Tucked in his sticky armpit, Emma dreams the flat silage smell of childhood. In the narrow box-room, Andrew's dream is a rosary of numbers, smoothed by frequent turning.

In the hallway connecting all the rooms, a cold spot spreads tendrils in the dark.

Emma surfaces. She tries to ignore the tug of her bladder and nestle back to sleep. It's more than cold that stops her crossing the hall to the bathroom. It's the texture of the silence, the thickness of shadows. The sense of trespass. She turns her mind to the problem of Satan in *Paradise Lost*, the importance of sunrise in *Ulysses*. Drifting, she misses the dawn.

Everyone is in the kitchen for Sunday brunch. Late morning sun blazes. In the TV alcove, Flo and Gabrielle are singing to Beyoncé. They play with words, juggling English, Danish and Indian-Ocean French. Rory has set up a BLT production-line. Andrew is cooking bacon with scientific attention, but his body thrums as it always does near Emma. He can feel her sadness across the room.

Emma is washing yesterday's dishes. In the unwritten law of flat share, the non-tenant girlfriend must pay her dues. Scraping burned pans makes her feel less of a parasite. Room-share with Rory has its own private price.

"The mind's its own place and can make a heaven of hell..." she recites to herself and feels something change.

Her hands freeze in the water. The hairs on her arms stand up.

The sun continues to blaze but all warmth is gone. A pressure builds, whining in her ears, and a hostile presence bears down. The soap-bubbles around her hands pop under the weight of it. She dare not turn around but she knows if she continues to stand there, she too might burst.

"I'm going out," she says. Her voice is too quiet to cut through the noise. But the four real-flatmates stop.

"It is a beautiful day." Rory agrees. Gabrielle stands up and turns off the TV. Flo follows.

"Seize the day," quotes Andrew with a glance at Emma, hoping she'll notice. He turns off the gas under half-cooked bacon.

A group outing usually takes hours to muster. Today, they're at the front door in less than a minute, coats thrown over pyjamas, feet crammed sockless into shoes. Emma hesitates in the kitchen doorway. The cold presence from the kitchen has flowed past her into the hall. She can see it coalescing in the corners, a sentient shadow between her and the others. If she doesn't move quickly she'll be cut off, and that frightens her more than anything in the world.

She steps into the hall and the invisible eye of a storm.

A vortex starts to rotate around her, drawing the stone breath of underworld up through the building. The walls push apart, the floor melts away and a fetid updraft holds her suspended, a plunging void.

If one of the others had looked back, called her name, she might have made it. But no lifeline is thrown. Flo and Gabrielle are already on the landing, Andrew hot on their heels, followed by Rory who slams the door behind him. On the other side, she hears them run.

Carried by fear, her body rails against the vortex, tries to push through. Static whip cracks through her, the air turns violet, something rips in her sternum and... she sees her body move away from her. It manages one step, two towards the door. She is screaming silently at her own retreating back, seeing herself stumble, drag into slow motion, degrade. Far away, her hand snatches at the door-handle and passes through it. She sees the panels of the door materialise through the fading body, as the momentum pitches it forward through the wood, to vanish before it falls.

The vortex slows. The pressure equalises. Walls and floor slip back into place, and the room is still. In the kitchen the sun shines, as if nothing happened.

She sobs airlessly, her weightless mind uncomprehending. Holding her face she finds her touch cold, her hands light as dead leaves. On her wrist, her watch slowly disappears. On the coat-rack, her biker jacket also starts to vanish. She runs to her bedroom. Clothes, books, laptop, phone. All gone. In the bathroom, her products have disappeared from the shower. She seizes her toothbrush, the last vestige of her non-tenancy... but her hand passes right through it. She tries to grab the shower curtain, a towel, the edge of the sink. It's like pushing quicksand, nothing to hold.

She sits in shock on the side of the bath. It's a full minute before she realise her rump is floating a micron above it, supported on thin air. She sits watching her toothbrush quietly vanish, from the handle up-wards.

The written word fades last. The postcard she sent the flatmates from Turkey lingers with "wish you were here". The dedication she wrote in a collection of Edwin Morgan poems hangs for a moment, like the Cheshire cat's grin, after the book itself has disap-peared:

"To Rory,
T W I N E
That
Which
Is
Next-to-nothing
Endures

with love from Emma."

"Emma" is the last thing to go.

To confirm her worst fears, she faces the mirror. Her clothes have evaporated, as has the skin that sepa-rates her from the world. Her form is the lightest shimmer of molecules held together by the faintest electric pulse. She is cloud, scent, shadow, memory. She is still standing there trying to trace her invisible outline, when the flatmates come home.

They clatter in, brazen with adrenaline and hearty café breakfasts. They throw coats where hers had hung, kick shoes into the space left by her boots.

Their vitality pushes her aside like a jellyfish in a bow-wave. They can't hear her crying their names or feel her sand-hands catch at their clothes. Their "collective hysteria" terror is already an anecdote, becoming sanitized by repetition.

She follows Rory into their room waiting for him to notice her absence. He hesitates for a heartbeat, perhaps feeling something amiss. Then habit drives him forward to the bag of weed stashed under the mattress. She float-sits on the bed as he rummages below, in the vacancy where her suitcase gathered dust.

"I'm still here," she breathes-without-breath, close to his ear.

She doesn't have the power to stir one hair on his head. He rolls his joint and lies back to enjoy it, on the bedding where that morning they'd had sex.

Is there nothing? Not one memory? Is even the smell of her gone?

As if in answer he takes the pillows from her side and adds them to his. He closes his eyes and inhales slowly, exhales slowly, then stretches out in a satisfied starfish. As his foot sinks through her invisible thigh she realises she hasn't just gone: she's been erased.

Numb, she gets up and floats through the hall towards warmth and familiar voices.

"So I'm not the only one who noticed something?" Gabrielle is saying, as she opens the fridge.

"Could be worse, could be cockroaches," replies Flo.

Andrew doesn't join their laughter. He's frowning at the mugs on the kitchen counter. He has laid out five. Two coffees without sugar (him and Gabrielle). One coffee with two sugars (Rory). One tea without (Flo). One tea with.

But who has tea with sugar?

She comes to his side, says his name. Touches his hand. Wills him to remember with all her strength. For a moment she does see him thinking: as if he's walked into a room and forgotten why. Then the kettle boils and clicks off. Andrew shakes himself out of it, puts the fifth mug back in the cupboard.

Her fury goes right through her gut, plunges through the floor to the tangled roots of the building, where a shadow fury bellows its reply, sends redoubled rage back up five storeys through the soles of her feet, out her mouth and into the sunlit kitchen.

It passes through her with a force to burst ears and shatter glass, but the room is stolidly unaffected. The plume of steam from the kettle judders for a second then resumes its upward flow.

But something has changed. She's plugged in, wired to a potent force, caught between worlds. A collective force. She is no longer alone in confusion, no longer powerless.

With power, comes confidence. Along with what she's lost, she discovers what she's gained. Liberated from her body she no longer needs sleep, food or warmth. Or gravity. The next few days are experimental, as she pushes the limits and possibilities of her new situation.

She finds herself strongest in the hallway, where the void revealed itself. As she moves away through the flat, the charge that holds her together becomes weaker, and with it her sense of self. She avoids the furthest corners. The front door terrifies her.

She can't interact with physical objects or make her voice heard: while her hand is too immaterial to grasp a door handle, her body is too solid to push through an actual door. Like a house-cat, she has to wait for humans to let her in. She can, however, float at will. She feels safest nudged against the ceiling, in the middle of the hall, where a steady thrum of connection replenishes her from below. After resting there, she feels stronger than she ever did in her material body.

If she pushes out with that force or charge, she can displace air. Using the same force, she can push a thought or feeling towards another person. Half an hour trying to communicate with Rory induces nothing but mild dope paranoia. Now disembodied, the things that drew her to him have faded. His oscillation between boisterousness and catatonia no longer enthralls her. The unkempt way he wears his good looks can now be seen for what it is: vanity. His personal habits don't stand scrutiny either. All her love and warmth has been replaced by one hand and an illogical two-girl fantasy, where Flo and Gabrielle use his manhood to explore their lesbian urges.

In disgust, she turns to the other flatmates. Flo is a non-responder, her antenna tuned to Gabrielle. Gabrielle herself is more receptive. She intuitively walks around the cold spot in the hall and a good mental shove can derail her train of thought, bring her to a stammering halt. To her surprise, however, the person who notices her most consciously is Andrew.

If she stands behind him and says his name she can make him turn around. If she touches his hand, he brushes the sensation away. She catches him listening, checking as he walks into rooms, contemplating the accumulating washing-up. Observing him she finds peace in his quiet, orderly life.

Today she's watching him shave. Her eyes follow the razor down a long upper lip, up a chin a touch too sharp.

He is not handsome. But she wishes it was her hand sliding across that sculptural face.

Her eyes shift to the space beside Andrew where her own reflection should be and, facing her non-existence, she sighs. Andrew stops shaving and looks up at the empty area beside him in the mirror, the space where she stands.

Can he see her? For a moment, it seems he's looking her right in the eye. Then his gaze drops back to the soapy water.

"I'm here, I'm here!"

Hope makes her desperate, pleading, beating the air with all her strength. She gathers all her energy, dark and light, to the centre of herself and pushes her full force towards him. In the sink, the water shudders. Andrew spins round to face her.

"Hello?"

"Andrew?"

Their words hang, flies in a web. A vibration holding its breath. She can see the hairs on his forearms stand up.

"Hello."

A greeting, not a question. She wants to respond, but she's used all her strength. She can feel the edges of herself bleeding away, the growl of darkness calling, its collective need answering her own. She has no choice. Whatever it is, it needs her to be strong. She returns to her safe place, recharging on the waves that rise from the sinkhole beneath.

In the bathroom, Andrew returns to the mirror and a world shifted off its axis.

Andrew not only studies science, he's defined by it. His thinking is shaped by method, analysis, constraints and controls. But physics is open-minded. Anything is hypothetically possible until disproven.

So he catalogues the phenomenon meticulously, finds ways to quantify the indefinable: the feeling of being observed, the invisible touch, or the implanted thought.

He sets up temperature and pressure sensors. He records the movement of a plume of smoke, or a paper lampshade turning in non-existent breeze. When the dots appear in the steamed-up bathroom mirror he transcribes them, looking for code.

She watches him. Her thought-fingers are bored of cold glass: she starts tracing across his shoulder-blades down his spine to the towel around his waist. She imagines tracing hip-bones. Feeling her, he turns with a raised eyebrow.

"Not all my sensors are remote, you know."

The voice is intimate in the cramped, humid space. He has no scientific reason for believing the "phenomenon" is sentient or gendered, but his voice gives him away and a lost corporeal echo twitches inside her. Hunger.

She leans kiss-close to his bare neck, feels the ripple of his charged skin and the blood rising under her breath.

"Measure that," she thought-pushes between his ears.

The scientist is no longer objective. Now, for his own sanity, he has to prove she exists.

He sets up motion-cameras, fishing-lines with bells, dehumidifiers, gyroscopes and magnets. The flatmates enjoy the diversion, tease the ghost-hunter, ask about his findings. But after weeks of persistent clutter, lab rules and no breakthrough, they lose patience. They blunder through sensors, unbalance experiments. Rory elbows "the spook lab" out the way.

Andrew vents to his captive audience.

"Whatever you are, you have an electrical charge. But it's hard to get a clean reading when the whole place is wired and full of idiots!"

The real frustration is with himself: the single biggest risk to experimental integrity is him.

His subject co-operates with the tests, trying to produce tangible results with intangible means. It drains her. She spends more and more time suspended on the hall ceiling, drawing strength. What she draws is more complex than electricity. It has a temperature and scent. It's a dirtier, meatier version of the thrum she picks up from the living humans. She never liked junk-food, so when the word "taste" pushes into her mind, she greets the idea as her own.

As the flatmates sleep, she passes her fingers through their skin to the charged beat of their veins. This living energy feels clean and wholesome. Flo tastes of the air at the top of a mountain, Gabrielle of triple-distilled vodka. Rory has a vegetable tang, like peaty spring water. Not wanting to be greedy, she takes just a little from each.

She doesn't touch Andrew. She doesn't dare.

As winter term shivers to an end, Gabrielle takes Andrew aside, concerned for his well-being. He's lost weight, she observes. He's sleeping in his clothes. She's worried about his studies. Andrew is touched by her concern, but he can't stop now. The readings are becoming more erratic with alarming spikes and blackouts. Each day he wakes up terrified his subject will have vanished overnight.

As Christmas approaches, the other flatmates leave and Andrew sets up for one final, mammoth data-capture. He borrows kit, books processor-time, runs cables and networks. She hangs on the hall ceiling drinking sour power. Rag-tatters of torn-up history rise like bats, violet sparks arc through her until finally, she is fully charged and ready for her close-up.

Spider-climbing head-first down the wall, she runs through the experiments like a well-trained agility-dog. A mind-push trips a wire, a concentration of matter triggers a motion-sensor. Her current leaves tell-tale cold spots in its wake. Steadily, sensor data becomes graphs, which become maps, which become rudimentary 3D models, rendered overnight to reveal an impossible sink-hole in the middle of the hall, and a shadow that may or may not be the figure of a girl.

Andrew is kneeling before his laptop on the hall-way floor. He's checked the data over and over and the results don't change. The phenomenon is real. She is real.

He is too exhausted to process the enormity of the discovery. All he feels now is relief that he finally caught her.

He lies on his back and looks at the ceiling.

He doesn't need sensors or analytics to tell him she's there, hovering above him, thrumming and supercharged. She descends and floats kiss-close above him. Readings go haywire as she concentrates her form against his body. Devices record his moan as she draws his breath into her, touches her lips to the jangle of his jugular.

Andrew struggles back to himself and sits up, feeling the heavy air of her lift. The rapid progress from haunting to experiment to courtship has flustered both of them.

"Sorry to slow this down, but…. I don't even know what you're called."

A joke, not a joke.

"Ouija". The thought lands in his head. For a confused moment he thinks that is her name, then the man of science laughs.

"OK. So that's the game you want to play. My turn to run the maze."

He draws the alphabet on a flattened cereal packet, puts the shot glass in the middle of the DIY board. He places one finger lightly on the glass but feels the push inside his head.

O

N

C

E

The glass leaves his finger behind. He is no longer the conduit, he is merely the secretary.

"Once upon a time..." As he scribes the letters a story forms, starting in the wide-sky flatlands of Norfolk and ending in the hallway of an Edinburgh tenement with a falling body: bookends to life of a girl who was always invisible.

It takes five minutes to tell and the full stop is a name.

E

M

M

A

"Emma". As he says it aloud he lightning-glimpses a girl – angelic smile, nose stud, halo of bed-hair- a subliminal frame in a film, spliced from another universe. Emma. A memory of the girl he wanted, always out of reach, lost, found and now his own.

Emma.

Between Christmas and New Year they weave their broken stories, each a mirror of the other's, into a single, spiralling helix of now.

isolated – alone
sensitive – hurt
taken - discarded
invisible - bullied

rejected – erased
seeking - found
saved – saving

The flatmates return for Hogmanay to find a different flat. The lab equipment is gone, Andrew has given the place a good clean and is groomed, rested and relaxed.

"Did you find your ghost?" ask Gabrielle.

"No," says Andrew, cheerfully. "But my data indicates a natural electrochemical explanation for so-called ghost sightings. I'm going to write it up for my dissertation."

"Great". Gabrielle has more important things on her mind, like opening a bottle of wine. The plan is to have drinks at home, head into town for more, up Princes Street for the bells, then on to a party.

But the weather has other ideas. A fierce wind blows horizontal sleet across Firth. By eleven pm the frozen flatmates and tag-on refugees blow back home, armed with booze, pizza, balloons, party horns and a case of indoor fireworks. Last through the door, Andrew smiles up at Emma: home before midnight, like a fairy-tale promise. She spiders down and floats with him into the kitchen, hungry to meet the guests.

By 2am the party has fragmented. Rory, Flo and a couple in skeleton onesies are attempting to ceilidh to 90's club anthems. Around table-debris, a drunken political debate rolls pointlessly. Along the counter,

Gabrielle lines up tequila shots for a row of mouths like hungry birds. In the TV alcove, Jools Holland is upstaged by a woman lap-dancing a man in a kilt: both are showing a lot of leg and potentially a whole lot more. On the other side of the corner sofa, a man strums a guitar while his mate sings a completely different song.

One cushion along, Andrew sits alone.

He is frowning at the man in the kilt. Or to be more precise, at the invisible girl running her tongue down the veins on his wrist. Kilt-man is too dazzled by the multiple electrochemical signals running through his body to understand. All he knows is his body is about to lose control in one of several ways, and he's enjoying it too much to care which.

"That's enough," says Andrew, across the guitarist. And then louder.

"Emma, you've had enough".

She's been tasting different guests all night.

The voices from below are urging her on, but the invisible girl somehow manages to let go of her prey and shimmy towards Andrew. She's so buzzed, he can see her outline as a mirage, shimmering across the room. If she had legs she'd be stumbling. If she had skin she'd be collecting mystery bruises.

"You shouldn't mix your drinks," he tells her, and feels her laugh ripple the air.

"Are you ready to party?" Her thought shoves into his mind as her mirage glides down between his knees. Hunger and lust pulsate towards him as she takes hold of his wrist. He badly wants the sensation he's been fighting for days and nights. Weeks. He's never wanted anything more than to give in to her, to be taken, right there. But he doesn't want the first time to be public and clumsy. It's a secret too tremendous to be exposed that way.

Gently, he turns his palm down on his thigh, protecting the wrist. He doesn't need to explain: she'll have heard enough of his thoughts to understand.

"I get it. Not until we're married." She lands a kiss on his forehead with a butterfly tingle. And then his impossible, magnificent girlfriend shimmers off into the party, making balloons dance in unnatural patterns for her sober physicist.

"Skoosh up!" Gabrielle butt-wriggles a space between Andrew and the guitarist. Her smile is wide as a lime slice and her breath 70% proof.

"Look at you, all glowing. What you get for Christmas, Andrew? The key to the fucking universe?"

"Pretty much," Andrew says.

Too brimful of it all to lie, he finds himself telling a part truth. He talks about a secret girl, how amazing she makes him feel. How work, love, and yes... the universe... have all suddenly come together in a way he could never imagined.

Gabrielle puts her hand on his knee, moved by his transformation. She starts to talk of her own secret love. The lover is not named, but it's obvious she's talking about Flo.

Above them, the being that-was-Emma spreads her tendrils through the house. She can taste the greasy dust on the top of the kitchen cabinets, the acrid gunpowder burns on the carpet, and the human sandwich-filling between. She feels Rory dancing with Flo: in the moment, enjoying body, life and soul. She sees him through Flo's eyes, his face flattered by half-light, lit up by his own laughter. She feels Flo basking in his attention, matching his dance and feeling bolder, perhaps even beautiful. The Emma-being dimly remembers Rory making her feel like that. Sometimes. She moves on before low thunder of anger becomes a storm.

Her tendrils taste other intimacies. Gabrielle's hand on Andrew's knee and her eye on Flo. She briefly mind-melds with multiplayer gamers in Andrew's room: someone loses a life. She eavesdrops on the chatter of the skeleton couple in the bathroom peeled down to their femurs: her peeing on the loo while he does the same in the sink. Their familiarity bores her.

She returns to find Lap dancer reaching beneath Kiltman's "Scottish Pride" and can't help herself. She sends one quick surge through Lap dancer's hand and Kiltman doubles over his aching, long-delayed ending. She laughs at her power, the primal relay from the dark earth. But she's not satisfied.

Something is snarling inside, drawn from deep below. Something beyond joy or mercy, beyond judgement or reason, with only one desire: survival.

Hearing the call she sobers, pulls back her tendrils, and realises the energy in the kitchen has dissipated. The music has been turned down a notch and Flo and Rory have gone. Where? She spiders across the ceiling, shark-floats the cold hallway and hangs before the door to Rory's room. Their room. Her room.

The door is closed.

She can't walk her whole body though a solid door. But she has learned that if her charge is strong enough she can stretch thin and light as smoke, and still hold her core. She folds her form to the floor, and seeps silently under the door.

The room is thick with skunk. Three smokers are propped against the walls minds scampering like grey mice: such easy prey her tendrils barely register them. She is after something meatier and finds it laid out on the slab.

Flo's on the bed next to Rory, sharing the wet end of his joint. While dancing Flo felt sober, but without the music her movement has lost all shape. Even lying down makes her head spin and she no longer wants the smoke she begged for. But she holds it down like a pro, receives a kiss she doesn't want. Having accepted that, it seems wrong to turn away the hands or the desire that Rory presses against her. He's suddenly much too close. His tongue in her mouth, his smoke in her lungs, his fingers up her skirt and under elastic, pushing between her thighs. He fills her until there is no space left for her and she absents herself entirely. From the shadows, mice-men watch with beady, greedy eyes.

What's left of Emma feels the stab of betrayal, and on its heels disgust with Rory. She experiences the potent lust and anger in the accelerating electrochemical exchanges of the two bodies. It throbs through her, along the hall, twisting round the guts of the house, descending four floors of hopes and hangovers, down with the shit-pipes to the dirt of the long dead. Their hunger for life at all costs bat-screams back up the building into what's left of Emma's mind. Ancient and famine-weakened, they want more, always more. If they are to survive, if she is to survive, she must supply it.

She occupies Flo, slipping into her like a glove-puppet. As she pushes out along each finger, each vein, she feels the euphoria of embodiment. Once again, she has breath, heartbeat, weight, skin. Inside the puppet-girl, she feels the man's energy too: the blood force that fills him under fingers, so close to her mouth.

"Feast!" The implanted thought resonates with desires so deep it feels like her own. "Feast!"

And with strength neither of them expect, she flips her victim onto his back. His eyes widen…

"Oh yeah".

… as she plugs into him and pulls his energy into her core.

At first, Rory rides the trip. For a while Flo is riding it too, relishing the kick of sudden empowerment. The dual intensity turns their whole bodies to conductive surfaces, connecting every part to the other. Remotely, Rory's brain thinks "Woah, so this is what it feels like to be the girl" before he is caught in the mounting wave of his own orgasm.

But it isn't his own. It isn't a place he's ever going to reach, because every pulse of his rising energy is being sucked away. The further he thrusts forward, the further he has to go. His heart is hammering, his body running to hell, but not only is he going nowhere… he can't stop. He's hurting himself, hurting Flo. But to his horror he realises he has no control over his body.

He looks up and sees a Janus woman snarling back. Her spider-limbed shadow is thrown across the ceiling by violet lightning. His scream is silenced by her descending mouths coming to suck him dry as flyhusk.

A coliseum blood-roar echoes from the roots of the house, blasts out through the roof into the wind torn sky. It's not just the voices of Emma and Flo, it's the voice of all the lost Undead, raging against helpless lives: invisible, hurt, lost, taken, erased in eternal half-death of hunger.

It's a siren scream of revenge.

"Emma!"

Andrew's shout, a blaze of light. The spider-beast flinches and Rory flash-frame glimpses a girl (angelic smile, halo of bed-hair) spliced from another universe. Emma. A girl he took, lost, forgot. He sees she knows him too. Too well.

"Emma, stop!"

The being-that-was Emma hears her name, feels a tug of humanity and with it, mortality. The scream of death rings in her head, the power of the body throbs between her thighs. But floating above both is something real and true: the helix connection twisting between her and Andrew. She grabs it like a lifeline and pulls. Static whip cracks, violet air rips, and she's wrenched out of Flo's body, away from Rory.

Suddenly, Gabrielle is taking the violated Flo in her arms, covering her exposure, holding her as she vomits horror and disgust, wiping her face and tears, and holding her safe.

As abruptly, the skeleton couple are two miraculously sober medical-students taking charge of Rory; checking airways and pulse, administering CPR. But the physical form of their patient fades in and out beneath them. They feel his pulse stop and start, his temperature rise and plummet. They fight their fear and continue to administer first aid as natural laws bend around them. It's their focus alone that holds Rory to the world.

Andrew can feel Emma above him, shivering against the ceiling-rose. Her fear and shame roll over him in waves.

"There's got to be something you can do." She's shaking her head, as petals of the plaster rose fall. "You're an energy carrier, right? You can switch the direction of flow."

"He shut the door on me!" shouts Emma, and the blood-roar echoes back a legion of fury.

On the bed, Rory has faded completely. The skeletons stand above him baffled. In a matter of heartbeats, they'll forget Rory ever existed. A beat after that, he never will have.

Andrew shouts at the ceiling.

"You loved him once. At least... he made you happy, made you laugh, right? That was you. That was real. Not this."

He takes in the scene with a gesture: the invisible dying man, the violated woman, the waiting skeletons, the terrified party-goers, Lap dancer and Kiltman trying and trying to get through to emergency services on the busiest night of the year. And beyond the circle of care, the thickness of ravenous shadows.

"Emma. You're being used, Flo was being used, by something... evil." His mind tries to swerve the word, but no other will do. "You have to fight it, Emma!"

A heartbeat passes, then another. The skeleton pair move away from the invisible body. Lap dancer hangs up her phone. Andrew himself is starting to disconnect, when he hears the whispering mice-men.

"Look. At. That. Are yous seein' this shit, like?"

"Aye. I'm seein" it".

"Woah!"

Above them hangs a faint violet light, a shoal of shimmering phosphorescence. As it descends, it forms a human outline. As she hovers over the bed, the violet glow casts the moon-shadow of an invisible man against the wall. She places her fingers against his neck as if feeling for a pulse.

Emma is imagining Rory dancing. She's imagining him flipping pancakes and kicking leaves. She recalls hip-flasks on Crammond Island and water-pistols on The Meadows. Drawing pictures in the soap as she washes his back. Reading poetry in bed and making up daft lyrics to songs. She remembers the good stuff, of light and laughter. And love.

Her light begins to rise and fall in slow surges, running from heart to fingertips, slowly filling the empty shape of the man.

When the paramedics arrive Rory is physically present, but mentally absent. The skeletons provide medical observations (extreme exertion triggering a cardio-vascular event). Rory is put on oxygen, attached to monitors and stretchered to the ambulance. His parents are on their way from Alloa.

The party disperses. Thirty suddenly-sober people gather their coats and file silently round an invisible chasm in the hall.

Later in the sofa alcove, Gabrielle strokes Flo's hair as she sleeps across her lap. Andrew lies on other leg of the sofa in companionship. They talk quietly, intermittently, waiting for dawn.

This night has changed their world. Beneath the veneer of civilization sinkholes of darkness defy time, space and even death. They are in the foundations of every city, everything men have built. One runs through their building. It's been feeding for centuries, its line of victims not just devoured but erased. Their husks composted into the hungry ranks of the Un-dead.

Flo squirms, fighting a dream, and Gabrielle soothes her.

"Is she in here with us?" whispers Gabrielle.

"No," says Andrew. "No, she's not."

The paramedics were concerned about Flo, but Gabrielle deflected their unanswerable questions, their cold instruments and blue lights.

"I can take care of her," she'd said. But now she's not so sure.

"We can't stay here," she says, softly.

"We've got six months on the lease. If we leave, we'll lose our deposit."

"Huh! We lost that when we let off them fire-works."

Andrew smiles, reliving the display he alone could see: a woman of violet light dancing among detonating, cascading sparks, like a God at the formation of a universe.

"Shame we didn't burn it to hell." Gabrielle's whisper is fierce.

They are silent for a long time, fretting the same problem. They could just sublet the flat and walk away. It's a good location, there'd be takers. But could they live with that? Leaving the sinkhole to take another victim, grow stronger, take another, the circle rolling on year on year without end.

"I'll stay," says Andrew.

"With her?"

Andrew shrugs. He doesn't have answers, but he knows he can't walk away from her. Or this discovery. This could be Higgs boson huge. It could challenge the Standard Model. The data he has now might be strong enough to get funding. With the right funding he could rent the flat outright. He could publish, maybe make enough money to buy the place. Him and Emma together forever, guardians of the sinkhole.

He looks down at the beautiful, terrifying creature curled invisibly on his chest, her being woven into his. In her sleep, she nuzzles his wrist like a puppy scenting milk.

He turns his hand over, palm down in denial.

Across the city, New Year dawns.

Anita Sullivan is an award-winning writer of theatre and audio drama, short-stories and screenplays who has had 60+ scripts staged or broadcast. These include adaptations of cult Japanese horror *Ring*, Pan Horror classics, *Faustus* and M R James. Several decades ago she lived with various ne'er do-wells in an Edinburgh tenement. Not at all scarred, she now writes horror and dystopia from the safety of a bungalow in Worthing. www.anitasullivan.co.uk

Paradise

Camille Bainbridge

"I am one lucky bastard!" thinks Mike. He takes a slow and lazy sip of his beer, flinching slightly as ice-cold drips of condensation trickle from the side of his glass onto his warm, tanned stomach. He takes a longer slurp and smiles widely as he watches Jessica walk confidently up the beach towards him. Her shapely body is gleaming after her swim and she looks better than ever.

"Last day in paradise, babe." he says, eyeing her thoughtfully as she dries herself off and adjusts her canary yellow bikini.

She pouts sadly in reply and bends down to give him a lingering kiss.

"Don't say that. I'd do anything to make it last longer."

Mike cannot believe his luck; she really is his perfect woman. Fiery red hair in a mass of curls, curves to die for and completely on his wave-length. The Spanish sun beats down on them and they lie, lizard-

117

like, soaking up the scorching rays. Mike replays their amazing week in his mind; seemingly endless days of sunshine and sea, nights savoured, sampling sangria and treasuring the breath-taking views. They have spent hours talking about their lives, their goals and their plans. He wouldn't usually go away with someone at such an early stage of their relationship but he feels Jessica is strikingly different somehow. She brings out something in him he has never felt before. He loves the way she listens to him, the way she kisses him, the way she looks at him. She has a passion and intensity that he didn't know was possible. An irresistible fire.

Mike is a bit fuzzy on the full details but Jessica's flatmate, Sara, had given them a good deal on her tickets, as she wasn't feeling up to the trip. Jessica had a very high-pressured job and said she'd murder for a holiday.

Mike jumped at the chance to share a spontaneous trip with her; to get closer than ever. Now they are having the time of their lives.

Jessica leans towards him, interrupting his thoughts, and licks her plump lips suggestively.

"Time for a siesta baby?" she says with a cheeky smile. Mike can't help but think he really is in paradise, as they spend their last afternoon feasting on tapas and on each other.

Their flight home is fairly pain-free; apart from the sharp and uncomfortable pang Mike feels when he realises how much he will miss their days together. He reaches over and envelopes Jess into a tender hug as soon as they land.

"I think I love you, Jess" he says quietly.

She flashes him a gorgeous grin and responds with a passionate kiss.

"Me too, babe! That's it now; we'll be together forever."

"Paradise." Mike sighs happily to himself as they collect their bags and head off for their train home together.

The journey passes in a blur of smiles and kisses and they can't keep their hands or eyes off each other. Mike can't wait for their lazy lie in together tomorrow morning. Jessica says he can stay at her and Sara's flat so they can fight the post-holiday blues together. They stop off at a local store for supplies on their way and Mike splashes out on a bottle of vintage champagne as a thank you for Sara.

"You soppy git!" laughs Jessica when he produces it with a flourish on their walk to the flat.

"What? We've had an amazing time and I thought it would be a nice treat for Sara to cheer her up." He ruffles her wild hair playfully.

Mike likes Sara; she is friendly and chatty. She always makes an effort to ask about his day whenever he visits.

"I'm not sure she'll be in the mood for champagne, babe." says Jessica with an unnaturally wide smile. "More for us though."

Mike feels a tiny prick of doubt in his gut at the lack of compassion for her friend. He shakes his head and quickly dismisses it. People say all kinds of things when they're tired and it has been a long day. He is looking forward to their night together and is unbelievably excited for the future.

Jessica shoots him a shy and sheepish look as she turns her key in the lock.

"I'm sorry baby. I didn't have a lot of time to clear up before I left."

"Sara will have done that!" He laughs and rubs her neck reassuringly. She pushes the flat door open and Mike is hit hard by a rancid smell. His blue eyes begin to stream and he fights the urge to retch.

"What the hell, Jess?" he gasps, "Nobody ever put out the bins here?"

"I told you I didn't have time to clean up!" she snaps as she walks into the living room. He follows her with a nervous laugh; she doesn't usually have a temper. He has never heard her react like that before.

His eyes are drawn to a large ruby-red stain on the couch.

"Did someone spill wine, babe?" he asks nervously, grabbing a cloth from the kitchen.

"I don't think so," she says in a strange, strangled voice. "You know I don't drink much red." She walks into her room to unpack and he hears her giggle to herself as she leaves.

Mike stiffens. He feels each and every hair on the back of his neck stand on end as he notices several long locks of jet black hair on the kitchen floor. He didn't know Sara wore extensions and, even if she did, why on earth are they flung on the floor? He begins to shake slightly as he kneels to clean up the mess. That acrid smell is hanging in the air, making it hard to breathe freely.

Something really doesn't feel right. Jessica is still giggling in her bedroom but he can't work out what is so hysterical. He needs to clear his head.

Mike stands to the open the windows, Stops in his tracks, when he sees a thick trail of crimson leading into the bathroom. He feels a creeping sense of dread as he begins to warily follow the trail.

Something here is wrong. Very, very wrong.

The smell worsens as he reaches the bathroom door and he suddenly retches, bringing up his last tapas. Fighting the urge to run, he slowly swings the bathroom door open.

He lets out an ear-shattering wail.

Sara. Well, she used to be Sara.

Her body lies crumpled in the bath; scalped, with large chunks of hair missing and deep-set gouges where her green and smiling eyes used to be. Her once-pretty face is now a mess of sticky congealed blood and, through a blur of tears, he sees thick slices of flesh discarded on the bathroom floor. Fetid blood is splattered across the walls and there are even rusty splashes on the ceiling.

From what he can see, Sara has at least three stab wounds in her chest. The bath is awash with sticky crimson pools.

His heart hammers in his chest as he sees *HE'S MINE* scrawled on the ornate bathroom mirror in blood. He feels fear snake tightly around him when he spots Jessica in the blood-stained mirror.

She is standing right behind him, a wild look in her eyes. As he turns to face her, she places a blood-coated finger over his lips to silence him and leans forward. She slowly removes the finger, kissing him deeply and passionately. Pressing her body tightly against his in the way he once loved.

"I told you I'd murder for a holiday babe" she says with a sickeningly sinister smile, before kissing him even harder.

"We'll clean up tomorrow. Do you fancy some champagne?"

Camille Bainbridge is a York-based writer, interested in folklore and things that go bump in the night. Her story *Make Louis Proud* was published in 2017 as part of St. John University's Terra Two project. She likes to add a twist to her tales and give her readers a shock.

Reverend Pea Pod & the Bloated Corpse

Ishbelle Bee

Boiled Shrimp Beach, East Scotland, 1876

Under the surveillance and squawk of a beady-eyed magpie, I stroll out of my rectory and down onto the beach. Oh rapture! Sizzle rays of delicious lemon sun zap me into delight. Energized, I leap into a mischievous skip. I am a happy Reverend! My foot squelches over soft sands and the swirl of seaweeds, those beauteous guts of mermaids.

But, oh! What's this? I spot an enormous bearded fellow by a rock peering down upon something bloated and green. I hurry forwards, approaching him nervously.

"Good morning my fine fellow." My eyes fall upon the greenish lump.

"Oh, Good Heavens! It's a..." I yelp.

"A corpse," he answers blankly. A crab pincer dangles from his wild beard.

"Is there any chance it could still be alive?" I suggest hopefully.

He stares at me, as if I am stupid.

"I think we can safely presume," he offers, "Since it's green and half of the brain is hanging out of its head, that it is dead."

"Yes, of course," I reply somewhat humbled, changing the subject with speed. "By any chance are you a whelker?"

"Excuse me?"

Oh dear, I may have offended him.

"Or perhaps a bag man of barnacles or squid gatherer?" I add rather quickly.

"I'm a Fisherman," he sighs, scratching his ear.

"I too am a fisher. Of men."

"I am not surprised by that revelation."

"What?!...NO NO no no," I blush, "You mistake my meaning. I am a spiritual fellow."

And I hold out my hand for him to shake it.

"I am the Reverend Pea Pod. So nice to meet you." He looks apprehensive for a moment, but then grips it.

My God! His clench is like iron. I feel my hand squeezed to its death.

Arrrrhhhggeeeeeehkkk!!!!! I squeal

"Nobbly Ned," he says, over my banshee shriek and, thank Sweet Heavens, releases me. My squashed hand flops by my side.

"Nobbly Ned?" I smile through the pain. "What a delightfully colourful name."

"It was my mother's and her mother's before her," he replies.

My grin remains fixed upon my face, trying to process the information he has offered. I am aware that rural folk are somewhat backwards and on occasion breed with fish or other family members.

"You're a big chap," I stutter nervously.

He looks blankly at me. Desperate, I focus upon the green decaying lump of flesh by our feet.

"Do you think you are able to identify the corpse? Perhaps it is one of your relatives?"

He stares at me with an air of disgust.

"Or neighbour?" I gulp.

He shakes his big head. "It's too bloated."

"Perhaps I should prod it with a stick to release excess air?" I suggest helpfully.

"How exactly would that help?"

"After it has deflated, it may reveal its true features."

"Could I ask you a personal question?"

"Of course, goodly Nobbly Ned. Ask away."

"Are you daft in the head?"

"Oh, you jest. No, no, no no. I assure you. I am quite sane."

"Of course you are."

I think perhaps he does not believe me. I look around and spy a pointy bit of driftwood, sticking out of the sand. Pluck it up hastily, exclaiming, "Here is a fine specimen!" thrusting it into the air, as if it were Excalibur.

I plunge it into the rump of the corpse

There is a low hissing sound

It explodes

I am thrown half a mile across the beach, landing head first into a sand dune. Well that was a surprise!

After half an hour of digging myself out, I brush my coat down, regaining my composure.

I scan the horizon, spying Nobbly Ned bobbing up and down in the ocean.

I wave, crying "Hellllooooooooooooo Ned." And spot a triangular grey fin slice the waters, circling him.

Ned is flailing his arms about and shouting. I cannot make out the exact words, although I would make an educated guess they are phrases exclaimed aloud in the ale house and outdoor privies.

He's screaming now.

Hurriedly, I wade out into the waters, in a vain attempt to scare the shark away by wafting my arms about.

Suddenly, Ned disappears underwater.

Standing up to my waist in the sea, I am frozen stiff with horror.

Oh, poor Ned! Oh, poor big bearded Ned. The sea is calm, a smooth line of grey. Oh Ned, oh Ned, oh Ned.

A seagull cries, piercing the air.

In a frenzy of sea foam, Ned emerges, heroic, gripping the shark. Head-butting the beast, who flops backwards, swimming off, dazed, in a zig zag motion.

"Hurrah!" I cry aloud and clap excitedly.

Sopping wet, Ned staggers out of the sea, his trousers ripped and falling off. Vigorously, I slap him on the back.

"Come back with me, Ned, to the Rectory and I shall feed you a mountainous pile of buttered crumpets. We shall sup hot tea and I shall find you fresh socks and a woollen blanket from the linen cupboard. We shall sit by a crackling fire, warming our toes, until we feel revived. You shall tell me of your people, whom I am sure are an honest bunch, if illiterate and unaccustomed to soap. You shall recite to me charming tales of your sea adventures and we shall laugh together. Oh, how we shall laugh!"

Ned punches me hard me in the face. I fall, dizzy, into a star shape on the sand - glimpsing him strolling off towards the village.

The remains of his tattered trousers fall off in shreds on the beach, revealing his naked and alarmingly hairy buttocks.

Ishbelle Bee has two entries in our anthology because there's not enough humour in horror. And because they're short.

The Nowhere Boy

Ciaran Laverty

J im leafed through the long-box and scanned the
covers of each comic book for something of interest. Some broke the five-pound mark. His
eyebrows furrowed as he was forced to dig further
and further back. Len looked over at him from behind
the till and checked his watch.

"You'll need to hurry up," he sighed. "We'll be
closing in a minute."

Jim pulled a comic out of the long-box. The title
read *Adaptiman* and the cover featured a hero in a
green and blue spandex outfit, looking off-page at the
potential reader, an expression of terror etched onto
his face.

Jim looked over to Len and held the comic up for
him to see.

"I never heard o' this one before."

"Adaptiman? Never read it myself. Some indie
publisher did it. They've been putting out a few one-

shots since they started but haven't done a series or anything."

Jim made his way over to the till and rummaged through his pockets for change.

"Well, a first issue's a first issue." He plopped the comic down on the counter in front of Len.

"That'll be three quid, then."

Jim prodded the change on his palm as he counted it out to himself. He rolled his eyes and looked up at Len.

"I've only got two pound." He moaned.

Len pushed a couple of buttons on the till and handed Jim the comic.

"Two pound it is then." He pulled a coin out of his pocket and took the difference. "You tell me if it's any good next time you're in here."

Jim tucked the comic into his jacket.

"Oh, definitely. Cheers, Len."

"No problem, man. Now go on, I've got to close up the shop."

With that, Jim left the comic book store and trudged home through a light drizzle of rain.

The street lights flicked on outside the front gate of his house. He shut the door, wiped his feet on the doormat, and hung his coat from the banister of the staircase. He could hear the television in the living room, through the wall. He wandered into the kitchen to find pots and pans had been laid out, ready for him to make himself dinner. When he checked the fridge, he found only a small amount of minced beef left in a plastic container and a tablespoon worth of tomato sauce in a jar. In the pantry was a handful of fusilli pasta. Jim gathered up his ingredients and started to cook.

He brought water to boil in a pot and poured in his meagre bit of pasta. He went back into the hallway and retrieved the *Adaptiman* comic book from his coat. He walked back through the kitchen and sat down at the dining room table.

To his right was the doorway into the living room. The sound of snoring began to drown out the volume of the television. His mother's arm lolled over the side of the couch and several empty glass bottles were strewn across the floor. Jim sighed as he took another glance over the comic book cover.

Adaptiman's costume bore no logo and the design looked as though normal clothing had been painted onto someone's body. On his head, he wore a red cap. That look of terror and Adaptiman's piercing eyes had drawn Jim to buy the comic in the first place but, now he was alone, it sent a shiver down his spine.

As the water bubbled in the kitchen, Jim flipped the comic open.

Within ten minutes, he had finished the book and his dinner was half-way ready. He scoffed as he turned over the last page.

"Waste o' two quid." He muttered and threw the comic down onto the kitchen table.

As he walked away, the back cover caught his eye. In huge letters across the top of the cover was the question:

Would YOU like to be a HERO?

He leaned on the back of his chair and inspected the advert.

Ever wished that you could have a story actually SET in a world where you're the hero? Well, prepare for an amalgamation of consumer and product the like of which you've never witnessed before! You could see yourself in the pages of our very next feature, as your very own comic book superstar! Simply send your name and photograph to the address below!

Palmotti Publishers, 61, High Street, Rochester, ME23 1JR

And if that's not enough, if you include a return address, we'll even mail you a copy of the issue completely FREE!

A free comic, he thought. And it'd be all about me.

He walked back into the kitchen to finish up his cooking. Scoffed down his dinner and went out to the hall to dig around in the chest of drawers where the stationary was kept. Once he'd found an envelope, he ran up to his mother's bedroom and took his most recent school photo out of its frame. He sealed the photo into the envelope, along with a sheet of paper where he'd written out his address. Before he went to bed, he scrawled the address of the publishers onto the back of the envelope.

He had twenty pounds in his piggy bank. He'd buy stamps at the post office.

He was going to be a super hero.

That weekend, Jim posted his letter. He marched home afterward with a spring in his step. If Len was serious about how unpopular the comic had been, then Jim was sure his letter would be the one to get through and earn him the free comic. By the time he got home, his mother was, once again, passed out. In the dining room this time. A TV dinner was sat beside the microwave.

Jim went to bed that night but couldn't bring himself to fall asleep. He stayed up for ages and thought up tons of different stories. He wondered if maybe he should have included at least one such idea in his letter. After all, he hadn't enjoyed the *Adaptiman* comic, so what if he didn't enjoy his own? While these worries began to set in, he felt his eyes get heavier and before long, drifted off to sleep.

He dreamed he was flying.

The Tuesday evening after Jim had posted his letter, his mother had gone out and left him a list of chores to have done by the time she got home. Washing the dishes was the final thing on the list. The clock struck eight o'clock as Jim dried off the last plate and put it in the cupboard. He peeled off the rubber gloves and tossed them to the side of the sink.

He would be up early for work the next day. Mister Duneen wanted him to sweep out the shop and clean the windows.

He decided he would go to bed early and had put on his blue and red striped pyjamas as soon as he got home, seeing no use in changing out of his work duds and into normal clothes.

When he opened the kitchen door into the hallway, he stopped in his tracks. A silhouette stood by the front door, too tall and slim to be his mother. A shiver ran down his spine.

The silhouette twitched.

He tried to swing the door closed and cry out for help, but before he could manage it, everything went black.

Paul leafed through the long-box and scanned the comic book covers for something of interest. Many were too highly priced for him, some even broke the five-pound-mark. He turned the peak of his red cap backward on his head, so he could get further underneath the shelves.

"Haven't seen you for a while," Len said, as he leafed through the previews for next month's new releases. "You been away?"

"Sort of." Paul replied. "It was a weird trip, like I was dreaming for a whole month. What's this one?"

Paul held out a comic called *The Nowhere Boy* for Len to scrutinise.

"Ah, it's the new one-shot from that indie publisher. Remember the one you got a while back? The uh…"

The Crimson Cavalier?

"Yeah, that one. Same guys."

Paul looked down at the cover of *The Nowhere Boy*. The hero was dressed in a blue and red striped costume. He was standing in a hallway, trying to shut the door, a look of terror etched onto his face.

"Well, the last one was pretty awful," Paul scoffed. "Plus, I never did get that free comic. Think I'll just be sticking to the usuals from now on."

He left the comic down beside the long-box. On the back cover was an advert. The catch-line read:

Would YOU like to be a HERO?

On the front cover, The Nowhere Boy was screaming.

Ciarán Laverty is a never-before- published, 21-year- old writer. While he grew up in Derbyshire, Ciarán now lives in the small town of Athy, Co. Kildare. He is a former student of NUI Galway's BA in Creative Writing. He owns over 600 comic books, and he's read every single one.

Skinner's Box

S a l l y   P a n a i

I woke with a numbing headache. Nothing unusual about that, except my hangovers aren't usually caused by my best friend hitting me in the face with a frying pan.

Skinner was sitting on the bed running thick coarse fingers through thick coarse hair. I squinted at him. Even that was painful.

"What the hell are you doing?" I moaned. "You could have fractured my skull, whacking me like that."

"Doesn't make any difference," said Skinner morosely. "You'll be dead by the end of the night."

Now, there's a disturbing thing for a best friend to say. I began thinking of him as my ex-best friend at that point.

"Don't worry." Skinner raised thick coarse eyebrows. "I'm not going to kill you."

I relaxed a little at that.

"Someone else will."

At this point I should have left. Stormed out. Even though it was my house. Instead I just sat there. It wasn't that I didn't want to take some positive action.

It's just that I was tied to the chair.

The room looked the same as always. Semi-tidy, except for a gloriously overflowing ashtray and several bottles of Jack Daniel's on my dresser. Even Skinner looked normal. Only I was out of place, trussed up like a turkey.

"I'm not going to hurt you," Skinner said generously. "I just want to make sure I have your attention. I don't want you storming out."

"That's hardly likely." I retorted, wriggled around for emphasis.

"Exactly. That's exactly what I'm getting at. This way you're scared enough you'll concentrate on what I'm saying and not interrupt like you did all the other times."

"Didn't know you were such an expert on psychology," I interrupted. I was mad and now I knew Skinner wasn't about to kill me, I thought he should get an inkling of that.

And what the hell did he mean, all the other times?

Skinner smiled thinly at my retort.

"Duncan. You have no idea," he said, enigmatically.

Honestly, you think you know someone... then they hit you with a frying pan and tie you to a chair.

Since I wasn't going anywhere, I took stock of the situation.

When you stay, like I do, in a wee Scottish village the size of Yesterfield, there isn't a lot of variety. Yesterfield isn't just a sleepy little town, it's positively somnambulistic. My choice, however. I'd elected to live here.

I arrived five years ago to get away from the rat race. Cities had begun to scare me. Such a complicated structure of tiny ticking lives, the whole thing seeming so big and solid and yet constantly shifting shape, minutely and menacingly.

Skinner looked tired. His shoulders sagged worse than the bed he was sitting on and his face displayed as many wrinkles. But now there was a hard edge to his look that I'd never seen before.

He seemed to be waiting for me to properly adjust to the situation.

The first thing I adjusted was my bum. It had gone numb. As I gyrated it around I felt the ropes give slightly. Skinner hadn't tied the knot tightly enough. That was good to know. With a bit of effort I could probably get loose.

Not while he was watching though.

I tried to work out what made this night different from all the other ones. It wasn't so easy tied to a chair with my head throbbing and my bum numb.

See, Skinner and I have a familiar routine. During the day he makes musical instrument, guitars and the like. Me, I run the local store. Most nights he comes to get me at 8.30 pm. He always arrives at exactly that time, he's very punctual. Sometimes we go to Yesterfield's only bar and get drunk. Sometimes we sit in my house and get drunk.

Tonight he arrived at 8.30 pm on the dot, hit me with a frying pan and tied me to a chair.

Skinner was looking at me again. He rubbed his head awkwardly. He seemed sorry for what he had done. Well... good. That, at least, was encouraging.

I was still scared, but I really didn't believe Skinner meant to hurt me. It seemed explanations were in order. I leaned forward and the rope loosened a bit more.

Skinner took a breath.

"We're both very intelligent men," he began.

Not a bad way to start, even if it wasn't true.

"You ever wonder what brought us both to this little armpit of society?"

Armpit? I always thought Skinner liked Yesterfield. If he didn't like it why was he living here? Mind you, I thought he liked me. Then he hit me with a frying pan and tied me up.

"I'm going to die tonight as well, if it's any consolation," said my ex-best friend blinking rapidly, "Only I'm not going to die in the way they think."

It wasn't any consolation. And who the hell were 'they'?

"Skinner," I ventured, "Can't you untie me so we can talk about this in a more relaxed frame of mind. Eh? Mano El Mano?"

"My name isn't Skinner" Not-Skinner looked nonplussed. "And your name isn't Duncan."

My heart sank. My ex-best friend, who I obviously didn't really know, and who wasn't called what I thought he was called, had hit me with a frying pan and tied me to a chair. I was beginning to realize he was a few pips short of the correct time signal.

Next he'd be telling me we weren't even human.

"Oh... I think we're human, all right," sighed Skinner.

Hmmmmm. He seemed to know just what I was thinking.

"I don't really know what you're thinking." Skinner smiled thinly. "It's just that we've had this conversation so many times."

Oh really? Well this conversation seemed to have slipped my mind. Maybe I was more blotto than I realised on those particular nights. I decided to try a bit of reverse psychology on my captor. Show a bit of sympathy and elicit information that way. Seen it on *Law and Order*.

"Let's start at the beginning," I said, as calmly as I could manage. "Go through this together. It'll help. We'll start with this...

...Who the holy hell are 'they'?"

"They are us, in a bizarre way, I imagine. I'm not sure."

That helped. Not.

"I mean you absolutely no harm at all, Duncan." Skinner seemed to want to reinforce my confidence in him. Then he took it away again.

"And I'm truly sorry for what's going to happen to you."

His eyes were bright but red rimmed. He sniffed.

"You're my best mate." He sounded as sincere as a raving nutter could manage. "That's no lie."

"The untie me," I pleaded.

"Not 'till I've told you everything"

"Jesus. Is what you have to say going to piss me off that much?"

Skinner smiled again, but not happily.

"It should. Oh it really should. But instead you just won't believe me. I know that already."

I shifted in my seat a little.

"Try me."

"I already have."

"For God's sakes, stop talking in riddles!"

I used the outburst to lean forward. The knot in the rope came within reach of my fingers and I grasped it. Now I could begin to work it loose. Slowly though. Very, very slowly. I didn't want Skinner to hit me again.

"You and I are clones… I think," he said. "Or something like that. Part of an experiment. Yeah.

Maybe even clones of the men who thought this whole experiment up."

I just stared at him. Couldn't do much else.

"Every night they kill us. Every morning new clones take our place."

My first impulse was to laugh out loud from sheer disbelief, but I submerged it. I was tied to a chair a few feet in front of a raving nutter. A few feet further away was the frying pan.

"Skinner," I said pleasantly. "I remember last night. You and I went to Yesterfield Inn. We had a few drinks. We failed to pick any girls up, as usual. Nobody killed us."

"Yes they did. Your clone from yesterday is dead. You are a new one, produced this morning, with a perfect set of fake memories, including your non-fatal drinking session with me last night."

"No wonder you had to tie me up, feeding me this nonsense."

Skinner reached for the frying pan.

"Mind you, I didn't say I wasn't listening." I gave a sneaky tug at the rope. "All I'm saying is that we could have had a theoretical discussion about this. Like we always have about things. You surely didn't have to resort to bondage."

"It's not theoretical. That's the point." Skinner clutched at the crumpled bedspread as if it were an anchor. "I might be a clone, but when I die tonight I'll be dead. Forever. O.K. so there's another clone here tomorrow with all my memories, but it's not *me*."

He jabbed furiously at his chest.

"This one. Me. I'll be dead."

His sudden outburst gave me the chance to pick at the knot and loosen it some more. All I had to do was keep him talking. Then, either he would let me go, or I would have the rope unwound enough to knock the living shit out of him. With the frying pan if I had to.

"We're part of some psychological experiment?" I said.

"One of many."

"How come you know this and I don't?"

Skinner had the decency to look embarrassed.

"You're the control part of the experiment," he admitted. "You're not supposed to have any idea of what's going on."

He glanced across at the bottle of Jack Daniel's on my dresser and blinked.

"For most of the day it's the same for me as it is for you." Skinner tore his gaze away from the alcohol and looked me in the eye. I stopped fumbling at the rope.

"During the day all I have are pleasant memories of the last five years. But, just before 8.30, every night, my real memory comes back. 8.30pm, every night I know the truth. I know I'm going to die before the end of the evening. Just like all the clones before me died. I have their memories too. That's a lot of bad memories."

This was a very elaborate fantasy and I could see where it was leading. Clever though. Difficult to disprove.

"Do you come and tell me all this? Every evening?"

"No, but frequently I do."

"And I never believe you."

"Of course not. You think it's an elaborate fantasy, just like now. Sometimes you humour me. Come up with logical reasons why it can't be possible. Sometimes I present the scenario as a philosophical argument, an exercise in lateral thinking. You like those. Then you try and help me think of imaginary ways to solve the problem."

"I take it none have worked so far."

"Nope."

"Why don't you just walk out of the village?"

"There's a double electrified fence three miles out."

"Have I seen it?"

"Many times. But we can't get over it and you always forget it in the morning. So do I, until 8.30pm."

"Why don't we dig a tunnel?"

"We can't manage it in one night. After they kill us they just fill in the hole again."

"Why don't we get the rest of the villagers to help? What about Jim and Doug and Mr. Harris?"

"They're no more than ciphers. We never really talk to any of them, if you hadn't noticed. The few strangers that pass through Yesterfield are probably just to maintain the charade."

"What about me. How do you know I'm not one of them?"

Skinner lowered his head and pushed his hands into his sandy hair. His nails peeked through like little cold eyes. I pulled at the knot again. Finally, he raised his head.

"I tortured you."

The hairs on my neck stood on end.

"Just one clone. A clone of you. I tortured you. I tortured you 'till you were dead. You're not one of them."

Skinner got up and poured himself a glass of Jack Daniels. He didn't offer one to me. No matter. While his back was turned I had unwound another strand of the rope.

"I've killed you a couple of times as well." My ex-best friend sounded almost jovial. "Oh... I've tried everything."

"All right," I piped up. "Assuming you're not insane, there must be a way out of this." Mention of torture had heightened my desire to be co-operative.

"I agree. I presume that's the test. But it doesn't help me if some future clone finds it. Nor you for that matter. We'll still both be dead by tonight."

Yup. That would seem the part of the experiment to avoid.

"How do they kill us?"

"Some kind of gas. Comes down at midnight. The locals seem immune to it. I cut a couple of them open but I couldn't find any answers there. Then again, I'm no chemist."

Charming. Still, I played along.

"Filters. We could make filters."

"We did. Every type. They don't work. Duncan... We've been doing this for two years."

He shook his head wearily.

"Like I say... we've tried everything."

Skinner stood up again. He had drained his glass. He walked to the dresser and poured another, larger drink. The sun caught in his tangled hair as he turned and gazed out of the window. Over his shoulder I glimpsed leaves gathering on the dappled gables of the neighbouring house. I wrenched at the knot, tearing a fingernail.

The bonds were loosening.

Skinner kept his back to me.

"There's only one course of action left, I suppose. I don't want to do it but I'm out of options."

"What's that, then?"

His shoulders shrugged, bouncing light.

"See, each clone wants desperately to live, me included. But, at the same time, I have these collective soul-destroying recollections. Two years of defeat and despair. They're not my memories, of course. Yet... they are. A cavalcade of horror unleashed with the tick of a minute hand. It's got to the stage where I simply can't take it any more."

I couldn't really argue with that.

Skinner took another sun-stained sip and gave a little gasp. I thought he had choked on his drink.

But he was crying.

I stopped pulling at the rope.

"If I were to commit suicide, however," Skinner said matter-of-factly. "If I were to kill myself tonight and every night. At 8.30pm. The very second I re-member what is really going on..."

He wiped his hand across his eyes, keeping his back to me.

"They'd learn nothing more."

Skinner put down his drink next to my empty glass and walked over, settling a trembling hand over my shoulder.

"It's a stupid gesture, telling you, cause I know you won't remember tomorrow. I just wanted to say I'm sorry. I owe that to my best friend."

He let go and stood back.

"You're not very good with knots, Duncan, are you?" He walked from the room.

"Skinner!"

I wrenched frantically at my bonds, tightening them. Cursing out loud, I slowed down and picked gently. Agonisingly. Deliberately.

As the last strand slipped from my wrist I heard the roar of my shotgun from the garden outside.

I woke up with a numbing headache. A proper hangover, this time.

Last night, after the ambulance had whisked Skinner's body off to Middletown and the police had questioned me, I drew my curtains on the vacant gaping mouths of Yesterfield's milling residents. I finished off the bottle of Jack Daniels. Then I drank another bottle.

I woke around twelve. To hell with the shop. I sat for most of the afternoon on the couch, staring at the pale flesh of the empty armchair and thinking about Skinner. I tried to grieve properly but that stupid psychotic predicament of his kept getting in the way. It felt like he had left me some sort of deathbed puzzle to solve.

I looked down at my fingernail. Still broken. Then again, if I was a new clone they'd just snap my nail before I woke up.

Stupid. Stupid, stupid. Yet still I sat. If I could have solved the puzzle last night, I felt my best friend would still be alive. I could have saved him.

The thought wouldn't go away.

The armchair turned from cream to ash and shadows gathered in its folds. Finally I got up, turned on the light, got a pen and paper from my desk drawer and sat back down

I tried to figure out Skinner's problem logically. I had one advantage he didn't have.

Time. Due to the nature of his fantasy Skinner only had from 8. 30 PM to solve his problem. I had all day.

True, I hadn't thought of a solution yet. Then again, my life didn't depend on it. If it did, I was sure I'd find a way. After all, there must be an answer. If I had all day every day, surely I'd think of a way.

Wouldn't I? Jesus. Skinner must have been terrified last night to do what he did. Out of his mind. Crazy mad. Thinking that his life depended on solving an insoluble quandary.

I tried to envisage the situation if it were reversed. If I thought the experiment was real. Jesus. Imagine if I believed I was the subject and Skinner was the control? How horrible would *that* be?

I smiled despite myself. If I was the subject, this clone sure as hell wouldn't have wasted his only day moping on the couch. Not if all I had left was a...

The bell jolted me out of my oppressive thoughts. I got up and yanked open the door.

There was Skinner, bottle of Jack Daniels in his hand and an expectant grin on his face.

"What?" he looked at my face in puzzlement. "I'm not too early, am I?"

I looked up at the clock

It was 8.30pm.

Sally Panai grew up in Scotland but now lives in Munich, Germany. She works in a fashion store during the day and paints and writes at night. She is half way through her first novel and has written several short stories but this is the first one she has ever had published.

Green Ladies

Keava McMillan

1 818: Orla

Orla pulled the shawl closer to her neck and hugged her packages to her chest. The carriage had stopped on the main street but, when asked for directions, the driver had simply pointed to the towers peeking out from a nearby forest and whipped his horses into the sinking sun.

The route to the house was clear. A thick, winding road starting in dense pines before thinning into a scattering of flaking silver trees. The house itself sprung silently when she turned a corner. It was the size of a church and the length of a street. It had more windows than stone and was covered with too many icing flourishes to take in at once.

Orla circled her new workplace, keeping to the edge of the trees and trying to find a door that looked inconspicuous enough to enter. Not the large glass ones crowning the twin staircases at the front. And the thick sets of doors under the archways looked too large, too central for use. A shape in a maid's uniform appeared in the blue haze of the evening. Orla shook the bronze leaves from her skirt and crunched across the path to follow the girl into an unseen side entrance.

The shape, who introduced herself as Karen, led her up and down the coiled staircases running the length of the four turrets that staked out the corners of the house. Each identical set of steps hosted little doors. Some led to the small rooms for servants and storage, sandwiched between the grand rooms for the family. Others let them flit into their domain, to clean and prepare without being seen on the main stairs and corridors. One opened into a bare room with cream walls where the housekeeper sat behind a large wooden desk. She stared at Orla for long seconds, taking in her chapped hands and curly hair. She frowned at Orla's low voice, an inheritance from her Aberdonian father and Irish mother, before handing over a folded navy and white uniform and instructing her not to speak in the main part of the house.

To Karen's unconcealed amusement, each circle up the staircase left Orla heaving for breath and disorientated. Tiredness mixed with dread at the thought of navigating the maze of the house on her own.

"What about the ghosts?" Orla asked Karen as they finally sat on their beds, brushing their hair in the last of the candlelight. The space hung between them and Orla almost missed the infuriating warmth of her little sister in the bed next to her. The house was impossibly big at night, aching and creaking as it settled down.

"What ghosts?" Karen moved the jug of water back to her side of the room and started to scrub at her face.

"Is there not normally one or two in an old house like this?"

Karen shook her head and drops of water shook across the invisible line which separated their territories.

"You just worry about keeping the housekeeper happy."

"No green ladies?" Orla asked.

"No green ladies." Karen said firmly. "Except for you of course."

Orla flinched and Karen pointed at her shawl. Orla curled the green wool around her shoulders and smiled shyly. In the past day alone, the shawl had kept the biting winds away on the coastal road, held her packages tight on the trudge up the stairs to her room and added a spark of colour to the worn navy uniform both girls wore.

Karen could tease as much as she wanted. The shawl would stay.

Orla slipped into the bed, trying not to wrinkle the clean lines of sheets with her inconvenient legs. The spluttering candle stayed lit on Karen's side of the room and Orla closed her eyes tight, hoping that she would fall asleep before Karen and the candle abandoned her to the darkness of the house.

2018: Frances

"What about ghosts?" An American couple stood expectantly, their grey hair blending into the cold walls of the dining room.

Frances shifted under their beady eyes, playing with the zip of her standard issue green fleece. She was only half way through her first shift at the country house and had fielded the question of the ghosts almost as often as she had directed visitors to the toilets.

"We're not really meant to talk about that." She smiled apologetically.

This was the first instruction she had been given after signing her name to the impossibly long contract that morning. Sweeping the contract, biscuit crumbs, and ghosts away in one practised gesture, the manager explained that there was no need to encourage that sort of reputation. Frances had nodded enthusiastically to exorcise the manager's worried glance at her studded boots and flowing black skirt. Mollified, the manager handed a cellophane parcel over the desk containing the moss coloured fleece worn by all stewards.

The Americans frowned. They had travelled to a real Scottish estate and now they wanted to hear a real Scottish girl tell them a real Scottish ghost story.

They waited.

"Well," Frances relented, as she had with every other couple. "The house was used as an internment camp during the war, for Italian Scots and Jewish refugees and the like. And the conditions were awful. Some people say..."

The American frowns deepened.

"Later in the war there was a prisoner of war camp here. The whole of this wing caught fire during a bombing raid. The prisoners and a Polish cook, I think, were trapped. One of the other stewards said he saw..."

The Americans sighed and suddenly seemed fascinated by a dull romantic landscape, squinting to see the name of its irrelevant painter carved into the frame. Frances shrugged and adjusted to a story, snatched from the tearoom on her lunch break.

"There is talk of a green lady," she smiled as her audience leaned in to catch each word, "A young maid, who worked in the house, died suddenly in a tragic accident. Some say she is still here."

Young. Tragic. Haunted. Each of these words electrified the couple.

"Oh my," the American woman fluttered a hand up to her neck. When she didn't find a string of pearls to clutch, she motioned for Frances to continue, "How awful."

"She had just started working for the family and was looking after the two little boys in the grounds. She lost the children and was so distraught that she tumbled from a cliff in the woods while she was searching for them. Some say she still walks from the cliff to the house, searching for the kids."

Delighted, the couple thanked Frances and scurried away. She was still smiling when she noticed the silent woman standing behind her. Her heart contracted.

"It's hardly a cliff. The closest we have on the estate is a big pile of rocks out by the icehouse."

"I'm so sorry." Frances twisted her anxious palms after the Americans. "They kept asking."

"Don't worry," the manager smiled. "They're not the type to come back with magic sticks or metal detectors. It's best not to talk about the ghosts, but the customer is always right and we need to keep them happy."

Frances started to smile but stopped when she realised that the manager never joked about visitor satisfaction.

"It's frustrating. I can almost believe the stories about smelling the Polish cook working in the kitchens after dark. But a green lady seems to come free with every historic house."

Frances gestured towards the corridor leading to the library.

"Wouldn't we have records if there had been a suicide?"

"Not necessarily. We know a lot about the families who lived here but domestic staff came and went without making any impact on the place."

Frances relaxed her shoulders as the manager moved noiselessly to another part of the house, to frighten a different steward. As the tension disappeared the ache returned in her feet. There was something frustrating about standing all day in a room filled with luxury furniture. Her boots began to scrape the backs of her heels. A silk damask sofa snickered at her from the other side of the room, a fine red rope marking its plush cushions out of bounds.

Two hours until the house closed for the evening.

1818: Orla

The children were not half as obnoxious as Orla had feared and nowhere near as awful as Karen had suggested. Christopher and Stephen might have looked like tiny gentlemen in their polished shoes and pressed shirts, but they had not quite picked up the aloof mannerisms. When the housekeeper and their parents were occupied in different areas of the house, they hung to Orla's skirts or frolicked boldly around the kitchen. They teased the cook and begged for treats like untrained puppies. They were not so different from her own sisters and brothers, so Orla relaxed when the three of them were not being watched.

Of course, in only a few years, the boys would realise that they did not have to plead charmingly for a fine piece. They could just order the cook to hand one over. When a spiteful rage held young Christopher in its grip, Orla could see the unearned power of the man he would become. Stephen, two years his junior, copied his brother's every move.

The little boys were impossibly clean but Orla made them scrub their hands and faces again before chasing them up the servant's staircase to the dining room, to join their mother for tea. The children's smart shoes barely touched the stairs as they bounded up to the middle floor. Her own feet were aching from a full day of standing and chasing.

Orla hissed at them to wait for her. They listened at the landing to check that their mother was ready before Orla inched open the door and ushered them through. She watched their little feet marching neatly to attention on the dining room carpet and waited to hear the lady instructing them to sit, before quietly retreating. She imagined seeing this from the other side of the room and wondered if the family ever got used to the wooden panels opening and shutting, as silent servants slid around their house.

The first time Karen had appeared out of the wall, Orla had screamed. As she heaved herself back down to the kitchen, she heard the secret door to the dining room open again. Her ears pulsing in case she was being summoned, she raced back to the door and opened it as smartly as possible. A surprised family stared back at her and she backed out of the room again, embarrassed. A figure stormed past her on the staircase, rushing from the upper floor with a bundle in her arms.

"Karen!" Orla gritted her teeth and whipped round to stop the other maid.

As the woman disappeared around the next spiral, Orla caught a glimpse of black skirts and a green jacket. The loose, disheveled black hair could never have belonged to the meticulously tidy Karen. Orla swung around the bend after the figure but, while the aggressive slash of shoes against the stone steps carried on, she could not find their owner.

"So you think..." Later that evening Karen fussed her blankets over her knees and stared at Orla. "You think that there's a ghost in strange underwear, following you around. And closing all the shutters?"

"No." Orla growled and moved under her own covers to change into her nightdress. "Well, yes. I told you. All the shutters to the windows slammed closed on their own!"

Karen propped herself up on her pillow and waited.

"Yes." Orla repeated. "That's twice I've seen her now. Really seen her, I mean. When I saw her watching me in the dining room I thought I was imagining things but today, on the stairs, she was so real that I thought it was you. She just shoved past me!"

"In her underwear?" Karen's mouth rarely deviated from a smirk.

Orla felt her cheeks flush, perhaps with anger.

"Her hair wasn't done up and she was wearing the green jacket and no dress... Just a black petticoat or something."

"I think," Karen snuggled deeper into her blankets and smiled at Orla. "You came here looking for green ladies and now you've decided you have seen one."

Orla looked at her friend. She was probably right. Karen had worked in these grand houses for years. She moved around the house with ease, touching and cleaning each old painting and fine plate with a confidence that Orla could never imagine.

"You'll get used to it," Karen said gently. "Soon you'll feel at home here too."

"Maybe... don't tell anyone then." Orla nodded. "About the green lady."

Karen grinned, raised an eyebrow that suggested her request came too late and blew out their candle.

Orla was left in the dark, feeling slightly foolish.

2018: Frances

"Hiding in the walls like mice?" The German visitor eyed Frances while his partner stuck his head through the door as if he might find an eighteenth-century maid sitting outside the staff room.

"Yes." Frances nodded, enjoying the shock of the couple who stood, solid and armed with guidebooks, at the top of the hidden staircase. "The architect placed all the storage and servants' rooms in the walls and in little rooms above the ceilings. That's why there's so much light in the reception spaces. They didn't need to close off a floor to make room for them."

The German couple sank deeper into the house. Their eyes flickered over the oil paintings and fine furniture but they looked behind the finery too, searching for signs of the people who had lived behind the scenes. Frances smiled at their disappearing backpacks. Most visitors were happy to inspect the surface of the house, a mix of snobbery and reverence stopping them from seeing the work, which held the illusion together. It was hard not to take this personally. Somebody still cleaned the floors, polished the windows, and stood by silently, ready to jump into action when needed.

The guests imagined themselves as nobility. They had a proprietorial air as they walked through the house. Backs hunched from year at an office desk would straighten as they imagined themselves lounging in the library of a man who had owned half the nearby town. This sense of ownership descended into bizarre behaviour.

In the past week Frances had politely stopped them from picking up silverware to inspect its sheen, running fingers along the frames of portraits to check for dust and sitting on French chairs, worth more than she would earn in her lifetime. Even hours of standing in the house and letting her thoughts stray did not produce fantasies of nobility for Frances.

This was not due to her sore feet or the cloying tightness of her green uniform. The house had a certain watchfulness. At times, when the skies outside darkened or she was alone was alone on the spiralling servants' staircase, this watchfulness felt supernatural. When the sun battered at the windows in the middle of the day, the eyes trained on the back of her head were those of her manager. Generally, she felt the gaze of security cameras that covered every room. The little black boxes squatting in the corners of the ceiling, jarred with the frilly stucco, which spread like lacy plaster fingers across every available surface.

The cameras told her, as much as any genuine ghost could have, that she was only here on sufferance. Their cold black eyes stifled any daydream of sitting casually at an eighteenth-century writing desk, or letting the hem of a long gown trail after her as she climbed the main staircase.

A thud on stone licked at the back of Frances' ears and she ran back to the closet door that opened onto the servants' staircase. Hesitant to leave her post, she peered into the winding tower. It would not have been the first time an over excited guest decided to explore the innards of the house on their own.

"Where are the couple who just left the dining room?" Frances released the button on her radio to hear the reply but white noise seared at her ears. She moved back to the staircase and repeated her question.

"On the third floor by the piano." The voice crackled clearer.

"Thanks, William." Frances returned her radio to the pocket of her fleece and relaxed. From his vantage point in the control room, William monitored every room. Even without his enviable, seated post - with a view of every interior - his long-standing role of caretaker gave him an air of omnipotence.

"Three more coming your way." His voice flickered through her pocket. "Last guests of the day. We'll close the shutters once they move to the top floor."

Frances waved agreement to one of William's many eyes in the ceiling and moved to the top of the main staircase, to guide the visitors through her section.

As always, the last guests took their time examining each utensil and piece of fabric on her floor. An elderly Canadian man squeezed every last penny of his entrance fee by grilling Frances on the lineage of the family. His wife simpered with pride at each new question while his middle-aged daughter grimaced apologies and tried to usher her parents on. Frances could feel her end of day smile starting to crack when the family finally moved up the stairs and William appeared by her side.

Closing the windows, despite signalling the end of the working day, was a task that Frances dreaded. It was time for the two stewards to move to opposite ends of the house and slam each set of wooden shutters closed, fighting with the bolts to secure the massive windows. On her first few shifts, Frances had assumed her unease would dissipate, as she grew accustomed to the lowering light of the evening, and gained the knack of forcing the bolts shut without damaging the wood. But the bolts remained truculently stiff in all weather and there was an eerie intimacy present when she was the only one in that section.

Frances and William turned their backs on each other and walked to opposite ends of the floor. They started with the smallest, most private, of rooms, dressing rooms and toilet closets, cramped by the additions of servants' quarters hidden above their low ceilings. Next the shutters closed off private studies and bedrooms. Closest to the main staircase, the inner set of rooms had no spaces concealed above them, their ceilings arched impressively high.

William was an older man with the long, thin bones of a bird and a nose painted by Bruegel. His bird bones did not stop him from getting to the last shutters before Frances and she bristled before helping secure them. She ran to the staff room before William and the other stewards could reach the top floor, scooping her bag and coat into her arms and moving back down the tiny spiral staircase. The last steward to leave had to turn out the lights as they moved down each floor.

She panted as the small servant's door slammed behind her, the checked her watch. Unless the bus was running late, which only happened on the coldest of days, it would speed off without her.

Frances slowed her breathing to long draughts of the early evening air and slowly followed the path to the town centre. She zipped her green uniform up to her neck and hunched her shoulders into the fleece. A wooden arrow indicated the icehouse, a few meters from the main path.

Frances stopped to peer into the woods. In her daily rush she had never strayed off the path to visit the little outbuilding. At her feet was a sharp incline with a small rocky path leading to a stone building, hidden by moss and vines. She stood staring down on it for a moment, weighing up following the trail to get a closer look.

Rushing to and from her shifts, she hadn't noticed the stillness of the forest before. The stained glass canopy of leaves blocked dwindling sunlight from the path. She shivered and moved quickly back onto the main route.

If she hurried, she might still catch the bus.

1818: Orla

"Count to one hundred." Christopher demanded. "Can you count?"

Orla ignored the little nuisance and started to count to ten, her hands placed theatrically over her eyes. Between her fingers she could see the two boys diving into the undergrowth. Squeezing at her lids and flailing with her arms as if she could not see them, she followed.

"Stephen, watch out for the nettles!" She called as the smaller boy disappeared into a clump of stinging plants.

The children giggled their way back onto the path to the old mausoleum and sped down the dirt road. She followed in their footsteps, still groping as if in darkness. They twisted into the wood of the estate and Orla hoisted her skirts off the ground.

There was little logic in the house hierarchy; the little gentlemen far outranked the housekeeper but, if the slightest tear or muddy stain soiled Orla's dress, she would be in trouble - whether or not she had been racing through the woods on the direct orders of tiny nobility. The last thing she needed at the end of a long day was to be burning Karen's candles late, mending her own clothes.

The evening haze softened the green of the trees. She would need to get the boys back in time for their tea. Orla recognised their giddy energy as that excitement that burst in little children just before the tears and tantrums of hunger and tiredness descended.

She whipped round, but the house was not visible this far into the estate. It was time to coax the little princes back to their castle.

"Ninety-eight, ninety-nine..." She shouted into the darkening wood. "One hundred!"

The boys giggled and their feet scattered onto stone, hushed whispers echoing around the woods. They were in the icehouse.

Orla followed them. She calculated that a few minutes of searching and bellowing would satisfy the children. She ran to the top of the icehouse to stampede the boys back home for their tea. A movement from the main path caught at the corner of her eye and she stopped.

It was not the first time Orla had seen the green lady standing in her shift, with that emerald jacket fastened up to her neck. But it was the first time Orla had seen the apparition solid, in the full force of her vision. Before, when a pale shape in green had flitted at the corner of her eyes, the shock had subsided with the disappearance of the woman - and Orla could convince her thudding pulse that she had been mistaken.

Now she could see every dent in the pale face and each thread of untidy hair. The ghost blinked two heavy lids ringed with dark smoke and the movement jolted Orla into action.

"Found you." Orla forced her voice lower than the shriek that caught at the back of her throat. "Back to the house, boys!"

The green lady still stood on the path, immobile, staring right through her. Orla kept her eyes trained on the woman and backed slowly towards the boys in the icehouse. The sound of her steps on the roof scattered Christopher and Stephen out of the building. She snapped her head around to check that she was between the children and the woman.

Her ankle swiveled on the green sludge of the roof and she fell.

On her back and below the gates of the outbuilding, Orla could no longer see the vacant eyes of the green lady. There was a sharp stinging shock at the back of her neck. She moved her hand up to the wetness but felt too tired to draw it back to her face. She stayed still for a moment, hearing the squeals of Stephen and Christopher crystallize into giggles. The boys were running through the undergrowth, squabbling their way back to the house. Safe.

She wriggled her legs. She would have to move fast to catch up with them. To find them and scold them gently for hiding so deep in the forest, and so close to the heavy gates of the icehouse.

A sleepy fog started to mist at the corner of her vision, heavier and more persistent than the Aberdeen haar. Orla would have to tell Karen and the others about her most recent encounter with the green lady. Surely they would not laugh at her this time.

She shifted again, searching for a hold to push her up and towards the children, the house, and the gossip of the kitchen table. Her arms refused to move and her head pounded.

She relaxed back into the moss of the rocks. Nobody would notice her this far from the house. She would stay still and rest, just for a moment, before launching herself back into the chaos.

Orla closed her eyes for a second.

Keava McMillan lives in the North East of Scotland and spends most of her time programming a small theatre and cinema in Banchory. She has a PhD from the University of Aberdeen and researches LGBT history. Her stories have been published in *Pushing Out The Boat, the Boston Literary Magazine* and *Black Heart Magazine* (no relation to *Black Hart Entertainment*) Her "Green Ladies" story is inspired by her time working as a guide in historic houses.

Happy Face!

Julie James

I t made me even sadder, when I tried to sing my
newborn to sleep. My voice was cracked, rough
and hoarse, from the long abstinence of laughter
and conversation.

When he smiled at me that first time, my lips split
apart and bled, accustomed as they were to stoic so-
lidity. Fused, as they had been, from bloody cold-
sores. I could only ever take the tiniest of bites. It
looked so dainty, you might think. So dainty! But not
for vanity's sake. For misery.

Eventually I decided I was never going to feel that
way again. But it was only recently that another cold
sore cracked open the side of my mouth, the split
bloody and raw. I realised belatedly, those funny
pointy little fleshy bits inside my cheeks - that I've
bitten accidentally so many times - might, actually, be
the edges of where my lips were. Rather than keep my
big mouth shut, not a good habit, I decided to encourage that rupture. Lip scrub, face cloth scrubbing,

stretching with cocoa butter and massage, peeling open my parched, miserable little mouth into the wide, generous smile that should have been there all along.

Results happen within days! An unexpected little smile cuts the edges of my mouth upward and I notice people noticing what is usually, clearly, too insignificant to warrant any attention.

It is working! Classical standards as measured by science prove that the faces humans find most attractive are often balanced on the phi, the golden number 1.618, the mathematical number of the universe. So, for the prettiest result, instead of my mouth being 7/8th of my nose, it's going to be the other way round.

I'm a bit concerned at this point. Maybe I should do an artists' impression before I make these, probably, irreversible changes. I stretched flesh tunnels in my earlobes one time. The lobes shrank back OK after going up to a 10mm tunnel... well, without an earring they looked disgusting. Not sure if my mouth will prove that elastic. I collaged an actress's nose on my profile once and it looked ridiculous! Beautiful on her. On my face, not so much.

All the sexy people in films have massive mouths, you noticed that? All the nice characters, the beautiful ones, huge! All the good and beautiful, all the kind and gorgeous heroes we elevate? They've all got giant gobs.

So I've stretched my lips, my smile right out, right along to those pointy little nubs inside my cheeks. The bleeding and scabby open wounds were not, to be honest, attractive. But the raw gashes, as I suspected and hoped, have filled out and fleshed up - giving me that wide voluptuous smile I craved. Even if it is a little lopsided.

My boyfriend has been looking at me funny. Like he can't figure out how I could have changed my face, without, you know, surgery or something. So, at the moment, he's trying to make excuses that don't quite fit. It's true, I don't have the facial muscles to support the doubling of my orifice. But the little bit of food or, whatever, escaping isn't really a big deal. And although the plump little rosebud mouth I used to have is completely gone, the nose on my face is actually not my most remarkable feature any more.

Isn't that great! Maybe my mother will stop kindly offering me nose jobs. I mean, why would I want to completely change my face in some Eastern European plastic surgeon's practice? Now I like my features the way they are.

A bit of lipstick and wow, my mouth is like suddenly my most attractive asset! Measuring my smile against my eyes, nose, brows, the proportions are pretty spot on. Not sure it's really wide enough yet, although it's stretched to pretty much where it ought to have been, all these repressed and voiceless years. I think if I'd actually been as happy as some of these bastards you'd be able to see my wisdom teeth, don't you think?

It's totally worked though, I tell you. You have to try it. They stare at me, like, all the time. I have the biggest smile in town, I so belong in Hollywood. This is my natural idiom. My teeth are so white now cause they get all the U.V. they can stand. It's true that my smile is a little off kilter. And the fan isn't an affectation either. It's not like I'm that hot all the time, but I can't actually stop the saliva kind of escaping out the corners, whenever I move my face. Just a blink or a twitch, the least flicker of a smile and the elasticity of my cheeks can't hold my lips closed.

They're so... long now. What used to be maybe two inches at most is now nearly five inches wide. When I talk, my lips kind of damply flap over my teeth, an undulating wave of quivering musculature propping up carmine fish lips.

People look, all right. But I'm pretty sure nobody's noticed my personal little issues. Perfect eight-inch lips. That's what I am.

I've measured them. I know.

Julie James won her first writing competition in primary school. The first ghost she saw followed her around for years. She has a degree from the University of Edinburgh in Anthropology and Religion, where she studied traditional Chinese Ghost

Stories. She has written short stories, a science fiction novel and a few songs which shall never be performed. She's a keen knitter, pattern designer, dressmaker, painter, and single parent of an only child who has had M.E. since he was twelve. Has a dog, two cats and toxoplasmosis antibodies.

It Was That Time of the Month

Roisin Burns

I t was that time of the month.

Echoing through my skull, a dull drumbeat woke me, which only worsened throughout the day. It reached a crescendo as Mr. Brooks managed to turn the marvels of the universe into a mind numbing hour of GCSE physics.

I stared blankly at the board but it was useless. My intestines had tied themselves into knots that would bring tears of pride to any scoutmaster's eyes. Unable to comprehend the simplest question I abandoned any attempt to focus. Regardless of the pain, I'd have been distracted by the stench. It smelled as though something deeply unnatural was occurring in my gut, yet it seemed to be undetectable to anybody else.

Eventually the shrill ringing of the final bell stopped the teacher's soporific drone. I think he muttered something about homework, as I staggered zombie-like out of the classroom. But he was probably used to that.

Then I got the text from dad, who was going to pick me up.

The car has broken down. I'm so sorry

I'm not supposed to take the shortcut, especially not in the winter, when the sun is already setting by the time school ends. Too many disappearances, too many mysteries associated with the thin strip of path leading between the fields, shrouded by a straggly row of evergreens. It was dark but connected one respectable suburb to another and hardly seemed dangerous.

Yet people whispered about something sinister lurking there.

Still, the pain meant I needed to get home quickly and the extra minutes shaved off my journey made it irresistible.

My footsteps broke the silence, reverberating on the tarmac, the echo unnerving me. I've always thought that footsteps have added significance in darkness.

Especially when you've stopped walking.

"Who's there?" Hesitantly, I addressed the shadows.

No reply.

Berating myself for being paranoid, I continued along the path, illuminated by the moon's benevolent glow. I was almost home.

The footsteps grew louder.

Fear threw me into action and I began to jog.

Whatever was behind me gave chase.

I broke into a sprint, breath catching in my throat. My muscles were aching as I pushed them to the limits of human endurance, but I couldn't outrun the pounding feet pursuing me.

They sounded like hammer blows, piercing the fog of my panic, reaching down to a deep, primal, dread in my bones. The pain in my gut suddenly increased and I doubled over in pain.

The footsteps slowed down and then... stopped.

I trembled in the cold night air, petrified. The hairs on the back of my neck stood on end.

Don't look round! Don't look round!

I tried to stop myself but, almost against my will, I peered over my shoulder.

A large man stood a few feet away, panting, eyes glittering in the moonlight. I could smell his sweat and the beer on his breath.

"Whatcha doing here on yer own, kid?" he rasped, advancing on me. "Don'cha know it's dangerous?"

The next thing I remember was running again, flat out racing, my panting breaths giving way to coarse, racking sobs. I pushed my body past its limits, ignoring everything but the overwhelming need to be indoors and safe.

The path, the way, the houses were a haze. I saw without sight, oblivious to the twitching of curtains and curious looks.

Finally home. But I wasn't able to open the door. I made one last desperate attempt to knock, but my hand slid down the glass, leaving a bright, crimson stain.

I woke the next morning in my own room. Slowly I untangled myself from the blood-stained sheets.

I *hate* it when I don't get back before it starts.

Padding across the hallway, I winced in pain, my distended stomach warning me to avoid breakfast. Still half asleep, I brushed my teeth. Washed the blood from my face and flossed the tenacious chunks of flesh and fibers still clinging to my incisors. I gagged at the taste, knowing that no amount of spearmint mouthwash could eradicate it.

Stretching, I heard the crackle of, recently grown bones snapping back into their usual positions.

I should be used to it by now. My parents always told me it was just a normal biological function, but it still hurts, this reshaping of my anatomy. Let alone the unpleasantness of waking up covered in someone else's blood.

I tell myself the guy was probably a mugger. Maybe it's even true. Anyway, there's nothing I could have done to prevent it.

After all, it was that time of the month.

Roisin Burns lives in Crewe with her family and enjoys writing poetry and short stories instead of revising for her upcoming exams. She reads voraciously and especially enjoys stories with a twist. At 16, she is by far the youngest entrant. In fact, she's younger than the official entry age. But we admired her go–for-it attitude as well as the story so we put it in.

The Plodder

J A Henderson

L ike rotting teeth surrounding a furry tongue of heather, snowy peaks topped black mountainous jaws which pierced the leaden sky.

God, I hate the highlands.

Worth the hike though. Impressive.

Didn't know that I'd find this spot again. Especially after 28 years. Thought maybe by now there'd be a car park built over it. Or an Ikea.

No such luck. The place still looked like hell with the fires newly put out.

But then, it didn't matter where I sat. It would come.

I lost my parents here. And my childhood innocence. Plus one of my brand new Puma training shoes - the ones with different animal tracks on the bottom. And my lucky toy rabbit, Harvey.

And this is the place where I found the Plodder.

Or, rather, this is the place where the Plodder found me.

I was a bright child, even if I turned out to be a miserable git. I used to make worlds in my head and me and Harvey played on them.

Well, I did most of the playing. Harvey was a stuffed toy, one the makers got just right. He was cute. Sickeningly so. Perfect amount of fur, eyes not too beady and the right distance apart.

I didn't want to come here, way back then, especially not with my parents. A chance for them to torment each other in a new environment, I guess. I was seven. We parked by the side of the road and my dad strode off across the heather humming the theme from 'Scott of the Antarctic'. I suppose when you grow up in Dundee you get a bit crazy out in the fresh air.

My mum hated outdoors. Being outdoors scared her. Mum was terrified of everything, except my dad, of course. She minced over the heather, skirting rabbit holes as if she expected a cruise missile to launch from one. And I'll give her that now, there's a lot of mysterious holes in highlands. Think of Loch Ness.

As it happened I found one that day.

My parents reminded me of animals that live in burrows. Mum was a cross between a weasel and a rabbit. Timid but vicious. My father was more like a mixture of racoon and sloth, but only if you combined the worst qualities of each animal. To be honest, I don't know that racoons have any qualities but that's probably what reminded me of dad. Except being stripy, of course, which he wasn't.

Anyhow, off we traipsed, over windy mountain passes the Great Blondell wouldn't have attempted to cross and, eventually, arrived at a beautiful, unspoiled glen. Unspoiled because you couldn't get into it without breaking your neck. My dad managed though, using the same mixture of bravado and cluelessness that got Columbus to the shore of the USA when he thought he was heading for India.

Eventually mum insisted that we sit down because her legs were all scratched, she'd only lasted this long because she was trying to outpace a swarm of midges the size of Oklahoma. My mum held an attraction for small stinging insects that bordered on obsession. She pulled an apple covered in wet crumbs from the bottom of her handbag and offered it to me. She'd also found half a packet of Tudor crisps, Sweet and Sour flavour. You don't see them anymore but Tudor were very innovative back then. She didn't have any juice, of course, so I went off to throw the apple at something.

"You be careful," she shouted after me. "There are lots of bogs around here."

My dad started to explain that there had to be a burn nearby to have a bog and how you could spot them by the emerald green patches on top, but I wasn't concentrating, as I suddenly found myself up to my armpits in mud.

My mum blamed my dad, naturally. I was her darling wee boy, so it couldn't be my fault and my dad began shouting that, for all my brains, I didn't have any common sense.

Maybe the highland air fuelled their passions, cause they had the biggest, blazingest row of all time. It was worse than being at home. I ate my crisps and tried to ignore them, which was a bit like Poland trying to ignore the Second World War.

Finally mum seized my hand and started marching me back in the direction we had come. Then I realised I didn't have Harvey so I started screaming and wriggling 'till she slapped the back of my legs. It was then she noticed one of my brand new training shoes had been sucked off in the bog, so she had to let father carry me even though she didn't want him too. Jeez.

I was struggling in my dad's arms and shouting for Harvey over his shoulder the first time I saw the Plodder.

Didn't half shut me up.

It was creeping past us, behind some dark hillocks tufted with sheep burrs, sneaking sideways with surging, shuffling hops like a hairy, dirty crab. It was thick with matted fur, inlaid with twigs and dead insects, dripping slime onto the nice clean heather.

I went completely rigid. My father thought I'd gone into shock, but he didn't say anything because it made me easier to carry. We got back to the car in record time. You know how fast people walk when they're angry.

And then my stupid parents made up! They decided to sit there in the car and eat Forfar Bridies.

"Roll the window up," my father said. "Or the meat will attract insects."

I begged them to leave. I said I wasn't well and that I thought I might be having an enema or cerebral parsley or something. My father told me to walk around outside and get some colour in my cheeks.

I couldn't, for I had seen it. Plain as day. Big and brown. Oozy. Crusted with thorny stalks. Boggy haunches blending into the earth. I had seen it.

And that wasn't the worst part.

It had seen me.

Eventually my parents poured the residue from their coffee flask out the window and wiped pastry from their laps. But it was too late. When we finally pulled away from the kerb the Plodder was only a few feet from the passenger side door and my voice had grown hoarse begging my parents if we could please go now.

They didn't listen, as always. That's why they died.

Because, by that time, the Plodder had my smell.

I realised this a few months after we got home. Home was Lochgelly, at the time. Lochgelly didn't have a Loch. In fact, Lochgelly didn't have anything except one main street that looked like its only function was to connect two sprawling industrial estates. Which, in fact, it did.

I felt the Plodder coming one Monday morning, when I was on my way to school. Double maths then PE, as if my day wasn't going to be bad enough.

I could tell it was moving slowly. Don't know how... I just did. Maybe slithering took the wind out of it and I guess it had to stay hidden.

I tried to think of a way to get my parents to leave Lochgelly. I mean, how difficult could it be? I couldn't understand why there was anyone living there in the first place.

All the other kids in town thought I was weird because I was quiet. Of course I was quiet, I had a bog monster after me. I even ran away from home once but, after I'd eaten my packed lunch, I had to come back.

Me running away caused my parents to have the biggest, blazingest row of all time - their swearing would have dazzled a plumber. It kept me awake as usual but that was good, for once, cause it meant I escaped when the house caught fire.

My parents were fried to a crisp. Sweet and Sour flavour.

The police questioned me for a long time. They wanted to know how the fire started. I told them mum and dad must have blown a fuse. They didn't think it was funny. But they couldn't prove anything.

In a way, the fire turned out to be the best thing that ever happened to me. The only person who actually talked to my parents was my dad's brother, so he took me in.

And *he* lived in Texas.

Suddenly I was on a different continent. Free from Scotland, free from my parents and free from the Plodder.

Texas was an interesting place. I learned to drive a Dodge pickup and crush beer cans on my forehead. Instead of growing up in a world of cigarette smoke and rain-ringed basement bars, I used to borrow my cousin's ID card and sip frozen margaritas in Chuey's beer garden, wearing sunglasses and cut off Dockers.

Then, one day, I felt the Plodder coming. Always knew it would. That's why I never bothered getting too attached to my new home and family.

It had walked half way across the globe. Edged out of Lochgelly, creeping behind low walls and through the bushes of suburban gardens, eating the odd pet to keep its strength up. Crawled over the stunted, scrubby, pylon pinned hills of central Scotland and through the housing estates of Glasgow. It probably didn't even stick out there. Then on across the dark abandoned ports of the Clyde and into the water. Out past rusted prams and floating oil drums, down into the Atlantic Ocean. Further out and further down till the light from the grey winter sky faded, particle by particle, from the water around it. Pushing through the depths, cold and black and solid as lead. Slowly, ever so slowly, inching the ocean aside. Heading for America.

Persistent bastard.

Eventually it reached the shores of the land of milk and honey, washed clean of heather and gorse and ready to pick up cactus thorns and Texas dust.

Me? Round about that time I began studying real hard. My grades shot up and uncle gave in to my sudden burning desire to attend college in Portland. Hell, the only reason I didn't apply to the University of Alaska was because I didn't know it had one.

The Plodder reached Dallas about the time my flight took off. I could feel it. At one point it was only streets away, probably hidden behind a grassy knoll.

I think that might have pissed it off. It only took two years to sneak its way right across the States to Oregon.

I quit school. Didn't see the point in being there anyway, as I wasn't career material. I bummed around the states but now the Plodder seemed to be catching up quicker and quicker. Maybe it had learned to hitch rides.

I boarded a plane for Europe. The Plodder took a cruise ship. Don't ask me how I know. Probably lay at the bottom of the swimming pool and stared up at the legs dangling down.

It was certainly figuring out how to travel in style.

And so it went. I saw the bleached blonde mansions of Italy and Greece; the black, sparse desolation of the steppes; the cloud busting peaks of New Zealand. And the Plodder saw them too.

I hooked up with women once or twice but, after a while all women want the same thing. And that was out of the question.

Then, one day, I realised it had chased me right round the world.

Fuck it. I went back to the highlands. I couldn't run forever.

It was time for a showdown.

I felt the Plodder coming long before I saw it but, eventually, the bastard hove into sight. Trickling like a brown, lumpy shit up the hill, stopping a few feet away.

It wasn't as big as I remembered. Only came up to about waist height. It looked like a chocolate drop lost behind the sofa for several years, only twenty times larger. The Plodder hunkered down beside me, or rather, it shrank a few inches.

And there we sat, feet apart. Me eating my sandwich in the style of a last supper, the Plodder dripping onto the powdery pumice. The sky had grown hard and grey and a bitter wind had sprung up. A billion tufted heads of heather, blue with cold, nodded angrily.

The Plodder stared at me. At least, I think it was staring at me. It didn't seem to have any features. Might even have been looking the other way.

It all seemed a bit anticlimactic, now we were face to face, or face to back of head. I felt a bit let down. I sat on my rock and the Plodder sat with me, like shipwrecked enemy soldiers on a thistly, bristling island.

I remembered something from my childhood about highland hospitality. How it was sacred or something, apart from the odd massacre. I tore off a piece of my chicken sandwich and held it out.

There was silence. Even the curlews above seemed to halt their high keening and hold themselves motionless in the air.

The Plodder shuffled around. He had been sitting with his back to me after all.

I motioned with my bit of sandwich .

"Go on. Take it," I said.

The Plodder didn't move. I put the bit of chicken on the rock and we both watched it for a while.

The Plodder heaved a sigh. Well... more of a shudder with a squeak at the end. There was another pause. Then he raised a gloopy arm and slowly stuck it right into his chest.

Eeeeeeeeeeeeh.

He looked a little like a hairy Napoleon which quite befitted his height and stature.

With a thloop he withdrew the arm again. In his hand or paw, or whatever, was a bright yellow object. It looked like a badge.

I leaned over to read what it said.

GLASGOW SMILES BETTER

All right...

The Plodder reached inside himself again and pulled another object out. It was hard to see through the mud, but it looked like a ticket stub for Ralph the Swimming Pig, Aquamarina Springs, Texas. He placed it on a stone next to the badge, not without some reverence, and reached into his chest again.

Soon there was a little pile of mementos sitting between us.

A room key for Beaver Village, Winter Park, Colorado. A table mat from Benny's Bar, Wheeler's Hill, Melbourne. A brochure issued by the Norwegian Land Commission, outlining irrigation improvements in the Hjeliak Fjord. A glass thimble from the Corrymeela botanical garden shop, County Cork. A token from the Tokyo Subway.

When you open your heart it's funny what comes out.

Despite the wind, the little pile remained unruffled. The Plodder patted it gently down to make sure.

I couldn't tell you what he was thinking. I couldn't tell you what *I* was thinking. The Plodder reached in again with what seemed like an air of finality.

With a quiet plop one last object emerged. It was shapeless, brown and covered in muck and looked, for all the world, like a miniature Plodder itself. But even under all that filth there was no mistaking those cute little shining glass eyes.

"Hello Harvey," I said.

I was surprised I recognised him after all this time.

I expected the Plodder to add Harvey to the random collection, but instead he held the tatty form close to his chest. Then he gave another sigh and slowly, very slowly, held my rabbit out to me.

I had a sudden tightening feeling in my chest. Or maybe it was just a sinking one.

"Are you telling me you followed me round the world for almost 30 years to give back a sodding stuffed rabbit?"

The Plodder remained silent but I noticed that he was slowly inching Harvey back towards his chest. I glanced down at his arms. The inching stopped.

"Listen," I said. "You've had Harvey a lot longer than me."

The Plodder nodded.

"I... eh... It seems more... appropriate if you keep him."

The stuffed rabbit vanished back into the Plodder's chest faster than any real rabbit ever went down a warren. He shuffled back several inches just to be on the safe side.

"Well," I said. "Haven't we been a few places, eh? Haven't we done a few things?"

And there we sat, looking out over the desolate beauty that was, and still is, the Scottish Highlands. Finally, I turned to my boggy companion.

"I don't suppose you've seen my training shoe? The one with the animal tracks on the bottom? I've still got the other. I have it in my luggage as a kind of keepsake."

It seemed funny to me somehow. One shoe had lain quiet and undisturbed in a bog all those years. The other had travelled the world in my rucksack. Neither had really been used properly. If it wasn't for the mud, you probably couldn't tell which was which.

"I could give them to my son," I said. "I mean, I don't have one. Not right now."

I shrugged

"These things always come back into fashion."

The Plodder scooped up the rest of his precious things in one fluid motion. With a long sticky gloop he rose and began to move off down the hill.

"Hey," I grunted, scrambling to my feet. "Where are you going?"

The Plodder stopped and pointed to a low jagged gap between two toothy crags. It looked kind of familiar.

"I'm on the wrong mountain entirely, aren't I?"

The Plodder turned and waddled towards his home. I buttoned my coat. Then, for the first time, I followed the Plodder.

Hell.

I never did have much sense of direction.

This is the second story in the anthology by Jan Andrew Henderson. But the book was his idea, and he runs Black Hart Entertainment and City of the Dead, so he gets away with it.

www.janandrewhenderson.com

www.cityofthedeadtours.com

ABOUT BLACK HART ENTERTAINMENT
AND CITY OF THE DEAD

Black Hart Entertainment runs, among other things,
City of the Dead ghost tours in Edinburgh, Scotland.
These venture into the city's legendary underground
vaults and explore the 'Mackenzie Poltergeist', the
best documented supernatural case of all time.
This is Black Hart's first foray into publishing.

So, it had to be horror.